SWEETHEARTS

SWEETHEARTS

A NOVEL BY
SARA ZARR

LITTLE, BROWN AND COMPANY
NEW YORK BOSTON

Little, Brown and Company

Hachette Book Group USA
237 Park Avenue, New York, NY 10017
Visit our Web site at www.lb-teens.com

First Edition: February 2008

The characters and events portrayed in this book are fictitious. Any similarity to real persons, living or dead, is coincidental and not intended by the author.

ISBN-13   978-0-316-01455-7
ISBN-10   0-316-01455-9

10 9 8 7 6 5 4 3 2 1

Q-FF

Printed in the United States of America

Book design by Alison Impey

FOR MARK

OCTOBER 18, 1998, 3:30 P.M.

A DRIPPING FAUCET.

Crumbs and a pink stain on the counter.

Half of a skin-black banana that smells as old as it looks.

If I look at these things and at nothing else, concentrate on them and stay still, and don't make any noise, this will be over soon and I can go home without Cameron's dad ever knowing I'm here.

He is yelling.

About how Cameron is always late coming home from school. About the lizard cage needing to be cleaned and how he knew he should never have let Cameron have a pet because this is what happens — children forget and stop caring and expect their parents to take care of everything and, well, how would Cameron like it if he came home from school one day and the whole family had moved and not told him because they were tired of taking care of him, the way Cameron was tired of taking care of the lizard? *I think we'll do that,* he says. *Maybe tomorrow. Maybe in a week or a month. You won't know until you come home from school and find the empty house. How would you like that?*

I'm not supposed to be at Cameron's house or anyone's house. Not without my mother's specific permission. But Cameron made me something for my birthday. He told me at school that it was too big to bring so he'd left it at home. I haven't seen it yet. Maybe he baked me a cake. The idea of cake makes me think about my lunch box and the two chocolate chip cookies I saved, and the Milky Way bar I stole from the 7-Eleven on my way to school this morning by slipping it up my coat sleeve while the cashier reached to get cigarettes for someone. I could share it with Cameron; maybe even put a candle in it. If he didn't bake a cake.

Leaves fall in front of the window over the kitchen sink. In a few weeks it will be Halloween. Thinking about what my costume could be helps me put Cameron's father's voice out of my head. The costume can't cost money because we don't have any. It can't be hard to make because there's only my mom and she has work and nursing school and doesn't get to spend very much time at home. It can't be anything from Harry Potter because Jordana Bennett and Charity Hays backed me against the wall in the girls' room and told me they decided that certain people could be Harry Potter characters and if anyone else, for instance me, showed up in a Harry Potter costume they would make them walk naked across the school yard at recess.

You know what I think? I think this lizard wants to go free. If you're not going to take care of it, it'll have a better chance out in the wild. Or if you're going to neglect it and let it die, why not just put it out of its misery now? Why wait?

I try not to imagine what Cameron's dad is doing but pictures

2

come into my head anyway, like the lizard being dangled by the tail or squeezed in two big hands.

A fly lands on the banana, stopping and starting in short bursts, and I make my mind go somewhere else again, to the kids I sometimes watch playing red light/green light at school. I've never played it myself, and they don't invite me no matter how long I stand just a few feet away wishing hard that one of them will. My mom says that if I want friends I have to smile and be friendly, even though we both know things would be a lot easier if we were Mormon like practically everyone else at my school. Anyway, who should I smile at if no one will look at me? Cameron looks at me. He's the only one who thinks I'm worth knowing.

Maybe I should get my coat and my lunch box off the living room couch and slip out before Cameron's dad notices me. Cam can give me the present later. I move as silently and slowly as I can, staring down at the pink sneakers we got from the secondhand store before school started. That's where we got my lunch box, too, which Jordana says is for babies. When I asked Mom if I could bring my lunch in a paper bag like everyone else, she said it was wasteful and more expensive in the long run.

The front door is just ten steps in front of me now. I pick up my coat and lunch box carefully, carefully, but the zipper of my coat brushes against the lunch box and makes a noise that to me is the loudest ever. No one comes, though, and I make it to the door. The knob is cool and I'm already thinking about my cookies and my Milky Way and how they'll keep me company on the walk home, when I hear the voice of Cameron's father behind me.

Where do you think you're going?

CHAPTER 1

SOME MEMORIES ARE SLIPPERY.

There are things I want to remember about Cameron Quick that I can't entirely, like the pajamas he wore when he used to sleep over, and his favorite cereal, or how it felt to hold his hand as we walked home from school in third grade. I want to remember exactly how we became friends in the first place, a definite starting line that I can visit again and again. He's a story I want to know from page one.

My brain doesn't seem to work that way. Most specific things about Cameron are fuzzy — the day we met, how we got so close, exact words we said to each other. There are only moments, snapshots, pieces of the puzzle. Once in a while I feel them right in my hand, real as the present, but usually it's more like I'm grasping for vapor. I understand that you can never have the whole picture; inevitably, there's stuff you don't know, can't know. But when it comes to Cameron I always want more than I have, would like to be able to take hold of at least one or two more pieces, if only because I'm convinced there are parts of myself hidden inside them.

Other memories stick, no matter how much you wish they wouldn't. They're like a song you hate but can't ever get completely out of your head, and this song becomes the background noise of your entire life, snippets of lyrics and lines of music floating up and then receding, a crazy kind of tide that never stops.

The memory of my ninth birthday is that way. Sometimes it's in pieces. Sometimes it's an endless loop, from start to finish. But it's always there.

I do have more memories of Cameron, things I know for sure, good and bad. Like:

The time we both got pulled out of class during the lice check and the whole rest of the year other kids called us the Cootie Twins.

The way he always got in trouble with our second-grade teacher, Mr. Duke, for not paying attention, for not sitting still, for having chronically untied shoes.

How us being together all the time made us a bigger target, the whole of our exile being greater than the sum of our outcast parts. How we didn't care because we had each other.

The three days Cameron didn't speak — to me or anyone else — after he missed a Tuesday of school and came back with his wrist in a cast. He still walked home with me, still sat next to me on the outside bench at lunch, a cheese sandwich in his good hand and between us the free cartons of milk we both got because of being low income. But he didn't say a word the rest of the week. I'd ask him questions and he'd shake his head no, or nod yes, or just look at me with big eyes. When we saw each other again on Monday, he acted like everything was normal.

I remember that Cameron made me feel special, protected and watched over, loved. If Matt Bradshaw came around at recess to call me fat and smelly, Cameron would fight him, usually ending up in the principal's office. When Jordana imitated my lisp or called me Fattifer, he stole her lunch and threw it away. One snowy day that my mom didn't get the laundry out of the apartment dryer in time I ended up walking to school in sneakers and no socks. Cameron took off his and gave them to me to wear. They were still warm from his feet.

And there was the ring.

Right before the summer between second and third grade I was in the back of my mom's brown Geo Prism, which was parked in front of the ugly building where we rented a one-bedroom apartment. Mom had gone inside to trade her Village Inn uniform for her nursing school scrubs before taking me to the babysitter. I remember that I had a library book about possums and I liked the way they walked on mossy logs and peered out from holes in trees and how their paws looked like little human hands. I tried saying it without a lisp. *Possum,* I whispered, putting my tongue behind my teeth the way I'd learned in speech therapy. *Mossy possum paws.* I'd be ready next time Jordana pointed to Sam Simpson and said, "Who's that, Fattifer? I can't remember his name." She made me nervous, and it came out *Tham Thimthon* no matter how much I'd practice at home.

I didn't want to think about Jordana, so I opened my lunch box where I knew there was a plastic bag half full of crackers that I'd taken from a first-grader's lunch when she wasn't looking. Stealing food was a bad habit, more of a compulsion really, and not only did I want a snack but also I needed to destroy the evidence, a process I enjoyed: holding the crackers in my mouth and feeling the hard, salty crunchiness dissolve into a slightly sweet mush. When I reached in my lunch box to get them, I found a small white cardboard box that I knew for a fact had not been there at lunch.

I slipped the lid off the box and lifted up a small square of cotton to see a ring with a silvery band and sparkly blue stone. Underneath the ring was a piece of paper that had been folded, folded, folded, and folded again to fit the box. I opened it. It was a drawing of a house with a fence around it, and a tree. Pencil-line rays from a round sun beamed down on two stick figures holding hands. Beneath the picture in a messy second-grade scrawl, it read:

To Jennifer,

I love you.

From Cameron Quick.

My mom got back in the car then, tossing her books onto the passenger seat and slamming the door. I watched her eyes in the rearview mirror as she asked, "Whatcha got there, kiddo?"

I closed my hand around the ring. "Nothing."

Other things I knew about Cameron:

He did crazy stuff sometimes, like tell everyone he was going to walk home from school without touching the cement. Five or six kids followed us the day he said that, watching while Cameron jumped from hoods of cars to fence posts to grassy parking strips until the space between the hood of the car he was on and a bus stop bench was too far and he missed, spraining his ankle. *Retard,* they all said, laughing. *Stupid retard.*

There was another time he stopped talking. He didn't come to school the day after my birthday, and then when he did come back, he was dead quiet for days. I felt like maybe he was mad at me, that somehow none of it would have happened if I hadn't been there and I wanted to ask him what his dad did after I left but I could never get the words out. In the end, we didn't say anything about what happened that day, to each other or anyone else.

The one thing you'd think I'd really remember is the biggest blank of all — the beginning of fifth grade, when he spent a whole week at our apartment. It was just him, me, and my mom, and I don't recall much other than that he was there and that I didn't feel alone for one second. We went to school together, came home together, ate all our meals together, watched TV together. It was like I had a real family.

A couple months later, he missed another day of school. I figured he'd come back; he always did. Then he didn't come the next day, or the next day. I thought about what happened on my birthday and was afraid to ask anyone where Cameron might be until not knowing felt worse than knowing and I couldn't stand it anymore. Finally I asked our teacher, Mrs. Jameson, about him, and she said, *Oh, well, he's moved, didn't you know that?*

What?

He moved, honey. Now go sit down so we can have current events.

I sat at my desk and let tears drip onto my notepaper while Jordana flicked staples at me every time Mrs. Jameson turned her back. *Baby*, she hissed. *Big fat baby.* What Jordana didn't understand was that she couldn't hurt me. Nothing could hurt me as much as knowing Cameron was gone and hadn't said good-bye.

Over the next couple of weeks I imagined all sorts of explanations, like maybe he'd moved to a place without phones. Africa, I thought, looking at the sepia-bumpy map of the world Mrs. Jameson kept in the corner. Maybe he was on a boat on the Indian Ocean. Or in an Alaskan snow cave, wearing beaver pelts and eating whale meat. He'd be back, I thought, to tell me all about it.

Soon I lost my only other potential friend, a girl named Gretchen who was new that year and had found herself eating lunch with me every day — and Cameron, when he was there — the way new kids would before they figured out who the outcasts were.

I'm glad Cameron moved, she said one day. *He was weird.*

No he wasn't.

Yes, he was. I didn't like him hanging around us. She picked up her cafeteria fork, prissy and delicate, with a sideways glance toward Jordana, trying to impress her.

You don't know anything about Cameron, I said to Gretchen. *So don't act like you do.*

Sor-ry. I didn't know he was your boyfriend. She looked at her lunch tray. *Did you take my brownie?*

You want *to be friends with Jordana? Go ahead.*

I'd picked up my food and walked off to sit alone. Later I took Gretchen's brownie out of my jacket pocket, picked the lint off, and ate that, too. She did get in with Jordana and her friends, and told them all Cameron was my boyfriend and we were both crazy and gross and he'd probably grow up to be a school shooter. The next couple of months, I was alone every single day at school, alone at home while my mom worked, alone alone alone, wondering where Cameron had gone and what I was supposed to do without him. The times Mom was home to tuck me in I'd ask her where she thought he was. Every time I asked, she'd get very quiet until she'd finally say, *I don't know, honey. I just don't know.*

Then one day at recess Matt Bradshaw told me that Cameron had died. The story was that he and his family had ended up in San Jose, California, where he always got into fights at his new school. That wasn't hard to believe, given the way he'd fought Matt more than once and stuck up for me with Jordana. Matt said Cam's enemies dared him to jump off the school roof, and he did. They said his jump cleared the school yard and he landed in the street. A car was coming; it ran over him. End of story. Jordana and Matt made a point of telling me about how Cameron's brains got smeared all over the road.

You're lying, I'd said to Matt. *You're a liar.*

Jordana shook her head. *No, he's not. My mom saw it on the news. Everybody knows.* She looked around to the kids who were gathering around us now. *Right?*

A few of them nodded. One said, *Yeah. Ask Mrs. Jameson. We knew a long time ago, but she told us not to tell you because she knew you'd cry, like you always do.*

It would explain why he hadn't written to me.

And he's going to hell, Matt said. *The outer darkness. Forever.*

The world around me got fuzzy. The last thing I saw was the

grainy image of Jordana pointing while she said, *Watch out, every-one, Fattifer is going to faint.* And I did. When I opened my eyes they were all standing around me, Matt laughing, Jordana curious, Gretchen looking a little bit frightened.

My elbow had hit the ground hard. My knee was bleeding. I started to cry, in front of them all, and no one offered to help me up or asked if I was all right or went to get an adult. Finally the yard monitor came over to see what everyone was staring at. I remember looking up at him for help, and all he said was, "Wipe your nose," pulling me up by my hurt elbow and escorting me into the school building, where they asked and asked me what was wrong, but I couldn't talk. I cried uncontrollably until someone finally called my mother and she left work to pick me up.

I asked her if it was true.

She said, *I'm sorry, Jennifer,* and sat with me, rubbing my back and bringing me cookie dough ice cream. Nothing she could say or do or give me to eat made me feel any better. I told her I was never go-ing to school again. I told her in the best words I could at the time that I couldn't imagine my life without Cameron Quick, without that one person who knew me, without the way he saw me and made me see myself.

She said not to worry, I still had her. As if having her had anything to do with anything. I'd *always* had her, I wanted to say, and what good had it done me? She told me I could take two days off of school but no more, that I'd just have to try harder to make some new friends. I rolled away from her then and didn't say one more word about it.

That night I held an imaginary funeral for Cameron in my mind,

with giant bouquets of flowers and big cakes and piles of little sand-
wiches and the Mormon Tabernacle Choir singing. He rested, peace-
ful, in his coffin, hands folded in front of him. Then I closed the lid,
because it hurt too much not to, and Cameron and all my memories
of him were lowered into the ground. And somehow I knew that if I
was going to survive, the person I was had to be buried with him.

CHAPTER 2

BIRTHDAYS ARE HARD FOR ME, AND HAVE BEEN EVER SINCE
my ninth. For obvious reasons. While other kids looked forward to
the attention and the presents and the feeling of being one year
closer to growing up, I always wished that October eighteenth could
be wiped off the calendar, permanently.

My seventeenth birthday was no exception.

In the moments between waking up and opening my eyes, I forgot what day it was. I ran through my usual morning checklist: what
I would wear, which books I needed to take to school, options for
breakfast, possible hairstyles and time requirements for executing
them. I didn't need to look at the clock on my nightstand to see
what time it was — I always woke up at the same time, my need
for routine humming even at a cellular level. It would be six, give or
take five minutes. I opened my eyes to double-check anyway; no
point in taking a chance. Then I saw it — a pink envelope resting
against the clock, with my name in my mom's handwriting and her
signature doodle of a smiley face inside a heart and hand-drawn
birthday balloons.

I turned my head and closed my eyes again.

Life needed a fast-forward button. Because there were days you just didn't want to have to live through, not again, but they kept coming around and you were powerless to stop time or speed it up or do anything to keep from having to face it.

I couldn't blame my mom for the card or the smiley face; she was just doing what mothers do. It's not like she knew what the day really meant to me. I'd never told.

And anyway, things were different now. I was different. Eight years had gone by and Jennifer Harris was as dead as Cameron Quick. It had been relatively easy to kill her off. I'd learned to stop reacting to anything Jordana and Matt said or did, instead counting in my head or saying the Pledge of Allegiance backward to make my face blank (. . . *all for justice and liberty with indivisible God* . . .). I'd started to always make sure I had clean clothes for myself even if that meant going down to the scary apartment laundry room by myself at ten at night while Mom was in class or working. I used three extra sheets of fabric softener to make sure I smelled right. I practiced my speech therapy until there was no hint of my lisp — *Sam Simpson. Sam Simpson. Sam Simpson.* When I was alone and bored and wanted to eat, just to chew something and have company, I switched from cookies and crackers to pickles, carrots, my fingernails, even little pieces of paper. I stopped stealing and only sometimes hid food.

Right before seventh grade, my mom married Alan and we moved and I was in a new school district where there would be no Jordana. I changed my name to Jenna so that no one else could come up with Fattifer as a nickname, and so that I could stop hearing it in my head. The resurrected me, Jenna Vaughn, lived in a nice house in the Avenues and had friends and a loving stepfather and a wardrobe in a normal size. She smelled like vanilla spice body oil and kept her hair conditioned and her cuticles trimmed.

Jenna Vaughn had made it. *I* had made it. It was my last year of high school and no one had ever found me out. I even had a boyfriend, Ethan, who picked me up for school every day and liked to snuggle and was only sometimes impatient with me.

The problem was that Jennifer Harris didn't always cooperate, and there were still days I could hear her scratching at the coffin lid, particularly on her — my — birthday. Like my seventeenth.

I got out of bed and gave myself a pep talk.

It's just a day, I thought as I loaded my backpack with books in exactly the order I'd need them. Just a date. A box on the calendar. A page in *TV Guide*. It didn't have to mean anything I didn't want it to mean. There was this one night around eighth grade when I was up late doing toning exercises, and I saw a motivational speaker on TV who said that the past only had whatever power you gave it; life was what you made it and if you wanted something different from what you had, it was up to you to make it happen. That seemed right — I'd made Jenna Vaughn happen, hadn't I? I reminded myself of that now. If I had the power to make myself into a new person, I could make my birthday into something new, too.

That was easy to think. My body told me a different story as I did my hair. October eighteenth was a thing I could feel in my stomach and fingers and at the back of my neck, an all-over sort of feeling that convinced me the motivational speaker was wrong. Life was mostly made up of things you couldn't control, full of surprises, and they weren't always good. Life wasn't what you made it. You were what life made *you*.

Mom and Alan called me into the kitchen to blow out the candle in my birthday omelet. I knew they wanted a leisurely breakfast around the table, familial celebration, bonding, etc., but priority one was pulling myself together before school, before Ethan showed up. No one wants an anxious, depressed girlfriend — especially not Ethan, who always preferred me when I was funny and in a good mood. And no one wants to hang around with a person who can't enjoy her birthday. I knew I was expected to be happy, happy, happy. Be happy, I thought. Just . . . be happy.

I set my flattening iron down and smiled at myself in the mirror that hung over my dresser. I'd read in a magazine that the very act of smiling stimulates endorphins, which rush in and make you feel better even when you're faking it. I smiled harder and waited for the good feelings to kick in.

There was a present on the front seat of Ethan's car, a Gap box tied with a white ribbon. "Happy birthday, Jenna," Ethan said, leaning over to kiss me, his lips cool from the iced chai he stopped for every morning. I opened the box and pulled out an orange sweater with a cream-colored stripe down the arms.

"Thank you. I love it."

"I know," he said, pulling away from the curb. "That's what you said when you handed it to me at the store and told me to get it for your birthday."

"I'm sorry," I said, holding the sweater in my lap. I knew he was just teasing, but I *wanted* to be the kind of person who could enjoy surprises. I wanted to be as spontaneous and free as everyone else seemed to be and not feel all the time like if I didn't follow some kind of specific map of daily life, disaster would be right there waiting. "I just . . . really liked it."

"And wanted to make sure you got it," he said, smiling. "So basically you're greedy."

"Basically."

I laughed. He laughed. We were on course. One thing I'd learned during my transformation from Jennifer Harris to Jenna Vaughn was that given a choice between being around someone who cried easily and someone who laughed all the time, people always take the laugher. So I'd taught myself to say the funny things that popped into my head and laugh at all the jokes. I had them all fooled into believing I was normal and well-adjusted, a rock of sensibility who could always be counted on to have a positive attitude.

We drove past Liberty Park and I pictured Ethan's car as a silver dot on the life map, zipping right along where it should. If you zoomed in you'd see that it was a cold and bright and fresh October day, the kind of day that, for most people, sang with a certain kind of hopefulness. I closed my eyes and willed myself into it, reminded myself that the girl in the car on the map in the hopeful day was me.

"Jenna? Hello?" Ethan poked my thigh. "Did you hear what I just said? About the play-reading committee?"

"You're meeting today after school and you can't give me a ride home. I know."

"What's the matter?" He gave me his patented Ethan look, one eyebrow cocked over mocha eyes that were always half hidden by light brown hair. It was a look that made freshman girls swoon and still made my own stomach twist pleasantly.

I flexed my endorphin-producing muscles into a smile. "Nothing."

At school, he walked me to my locker, which Katy and Steph had decorated with peach-colored wrapping paper and gold ribbon. I projected a reasonable facsimile of surprised glee, even though Katy and Steph weren't actually there and couldn't see me. It would be good practice for later, when I knew everyone in homeroom would sing "Happy Birthday" and Mr. Moran would make me stand in front and get handshakes and hugs from a receiving line made up of the whole senior class — all sixteen of us. We were the first graduating class of Jones Hall, a small charter school for kids who were too smart or too creative — or too non-Mormon, even though no one ever said it — to cope in the regular Salt Lake City schools. The birthday parade was one of the little traditions Mr. Moran had started with us our freshman year.

I gathered up the cards from my locker and Ethan put his arm around my shoulders, bumping against me as he walked his bouncy walk in his signature red high-tops, hair flopping cutely over one side of his face. I experienced a moment of contentment then, the kind I'd have every so often when I felt completely like Jenna Vaughn and truly believed that she was me and I was her.

Ethan and I were on our third month of official couplehood, which had started with an end-of-summer accidental date at the main library. "Hey, Jenna, what are you doing here?" "Checking out books, oddly enough." "Believe it or not, so am I!" It was hard to believe I had a boyfriend at all, let alone the kind of boyfriend other girls wanted. But he was mine; he'd picked me. Me, Jennifer Harris.

Actually, he'd picked Jenna Vaughn.

Ethan didn't know anything about the fat girl, the Cootie Twin, the loner and reject. The only person who had ever picked Jennifer Harris was Cameron Quick, and sometimes when I was with Ethan I felt the smallest twinge of guilt, like being with him was a betrayal. The one thing that could never die or be buried was my loyalty to Cameron for everything he'd done for me and what we'd been through together, even if that loyalty was to a ghost.

By lunch, the work of being the birthday version of Jenna Vaughn started to wear on me. I'd been smiling all morning at the Happy Birthdays and the hugs and compliments while Jennifer Harris dogged me. I kept looking over my shoulder for I don't know what, and hearing Cameron's dad's voice: *Where do you think you're going?*

"Jenna. J.V.? I asked what your parents got you." Katy was jiggling her legs the way she always did. It shook the whole table and drove us crazy, but we generally didn't say anything. All of us were at Jones for *some* kind of Issue, which made us pretty tolerant. For Katy, it was ADHD and some anger management stuff that we really tried not to tease her about. Steph had a learning disability that went undiagnosed until eighth grade, when she was already too far behind to catch up in a regular school; also she had a habit of "dating" every boy in school, which could cause problems. Ethan was some kind of creative genius and everything bored him. As for me, even after making some good progress in junior high, teachers complained I lived too much in my head instead of the real world and Mom thought the smaller class size at Jones would help me stay focused.

I answered Katy: "Nothing yet."

"What do you think they're going to get you?"

"I don't know." I knew this would not be an acceptable answer to Katy, especially since I'd in no way tried to make it witty.

She let her skinny, freckled arms fall on the table with an exasperated thwack. "Can't you take a *guess?*"

"Katy," Steph said, "she just said she doesn't know. Maybe she wants to be surprised."

Ethan laughed. "No. She definitely doesn't want to be surprised. She hates surprises."

"Oh, yeah? I've got a surprise right here." Gil Guerrero leaped onto the cafeteria bench and began to belt out "Sixteen Going on Seventeen" from *The Sound of Music.* Everyone turned and stared with slightly horrified and annoyed expressions — Jones Hall might have been special, but it wasn't exactly the set of *Fame.* We were still in Utah, after all. I buried my head in my hands and laughed because that's what you're supposed to do when you are being affectionately humiliated by friends — or so I'd observed in movies and TV.

"Gil," Steph said, "is that really necessary?" I peeked through my fingers. Steph was licking frosting off a cupcake in her shamelessly sexy way, gazing up at Gil, who had stopped singing and was now staring at her. "And are you looking down my shirt?" she asked him.

He jumped down off the bench. "No."

Steph changed the subject to the play-reading committee. With the attention safely off me, I tuned them out to eat my lunch: half a sandwich, a low-fat yogurt, and a small peanut butter cookie. I slid the cookie over to Ethan, guilty about the cheese in my omelet that morning. I'd spent too many hours hiking the hills of the Avenues, running up City Creek Canyon, and doing late-night crunches to let one pound of Fattifer back into my life. I smashed up the last quarter of my sandwich and stuffed it in my lunch bag. Even though the day was nearly half over and nothing bad had happened, it couldn't hurt to hurry it along. "Let's go to trig early," I told Katy. "Maybe we'll actually learn something."

CHAPTER 3

WHERE DO YOU THINK YOU'RE GOING?

I turn to see him, Cameron's dad. He is tall, a lot taller than my mom and most of the teachers at school, and has Cameron's big eyes.

I recognize you, he says, studying me with a smile. *You're Cam's little girlfriend. He's got a picture of you in his room.*

He sounds nicer now. Maybe he's just a regular dad, maybe what I heard him saying to Cameron before wasn't really mean, maybe it was like a joke. I don't know how fathers are. Mine's been gone since I was two years old. Maybe they are like this — a little scary and big but mostly teasing.

But then he says: *I guess my little guy is a chubby chaser, huh? Well at least he's not a fairy.*

Tears come to my eyes and my face is hot. I pull the hem of my T-shirt down to cover the part of my stomach that always pokes out, white and lumpy. It's baby fat, my mom says, baby fat that is also on the tops of my knees and inside my thighs that rub together and under my chin. She says I'll grow out of it.

I don't want to be here. It's only one step to the door. And then Cameron is standing there, behind his father, looking at me and I can't leave him. I can't leave him here alone.

A noise startled me out of my daydream-slash-memory. It was someone coming home, either my mom or Alan. My breathing had gotten quicker; sweat prickled on my forehead. I sat up and pulled myself together so that when Alan knocked on my bedroom door I was ready to say, "Come in."

He stuck his head in the room. "Hiya. I've got something for you out here." He stared, and came farther into the room. "If this is a good time. You look a little pale."

"It's fine," I said, making my voice steady. "I guess I fell asleep or something." When I'd gotten home from school, my face hurt from smiling and there was a headache developing behind my left eye. Katy had given me a ride home since Steph and Ethan had play-reading committee, and she spent the whole time on a stream-of-consciousness rant on Jones Hall boys ("There aren't nearly enough of them . . . haven't you noticed the grossly imbalanced boy/girl ratio?") and the trouble with drugstore makeup ("It's hell being a red-head, Jenna, you don't know."). I'd nodded and laughed and added my opinion when she stopped to take a breath, but even in her advanced state of self-absorption she'd looked over at me at one point to say, "You don't seem like yourself today, you know."

"I don't?"

"Nope."

I'd joked: "Who do I seem like?"

"No one *I* know."

My smile froze, but Katy didn't notice, moving on to her next topic while I sat in silence for the rest of the ride. Now, I got up and followed Alan into the kitchen, staying close to the wake of calmness that always surrounded him. He's like a walking security blanket — quiet voice, softly curling gray hair, unassertive wire-rim glasses. I'm sure his general aura of safety had a lot, or everything, to do with why my mom accepted his proposal after only three dates.

"Well." He turned to me. "I drove an old Ford Escort home from work today, instead of the Subaru."

I waited for more.

"You might be asking yourself why I would do that." He leaned toward me and lowered his voice. "This is your cue to ask me why I would do that."

"Why," I said, playing along, "would you do that?"

"I'm so glad you asked!" He placed a key on the counter with a flourish. "It's yours."

"What?" I had to take a second to drag my mind from Cameron's nine-year-old bedroom to my seventeen-year-old kitchen.

"Don't get too excited. It's a hideous shade of green. But happy birthday."

I picked up the key. This was a good surprise — a good surprise was happening to me. I decided to take it as a sign that things were going to be different this year, and hugged Alan. "Thank you. Thank you!" I let him go. "It's from you and Mom?"

"She knows about it. As of about an hour ago when I called to

24

break the news." He sorted through the stack of mail on the counter. "One of the new adjuncts posted it on the intranet today and I thought I'd better snap it up before someone else did."

"Thank you so, so much."

"Why don't you drive it around the block before you go thanking me excessively. It might be a lemon."

"If you insist."

I ran outside and got behind the wheel. The car had the faintest smell of spilled coffee and a tear in the passenger seat fabric, but to me it was perfect. After fixing all the radio presets, I cruised down the hill a few blocks, then up again. I imagined driving it to Katy's later, then we'd pick up Steph and go out somewhere and stay late and make trouble and I'd be my Jenna Vaughn self and this would be my new birthday memory.

At the corner of K Street and Fourth Avenue, I slowed down to let a pedestrian cross, a boy around my age. Maybe because he was so tall or maybe because of the way he walked — with a determined leaning into the cold — I couldn't take my eyes off him. His face was angled away from the car, and I got this strange urge to make him turn around so I could see it. I pressed my hand to the horn, but no sound came out, which was a relief. What was I thinking, anyway, doing something weird and embarrassing like honking at a stranger? Just then my cell phone rang from the pocket of my jacket. I pulled the car over, saw it was Ethan, and answered.

"Hi," I said, still watching the figure go down the street. "Guess what?"

"What? You got all your trig homework done?"

"No. Think more within the realm of possibility."

"You got a tattoo?"

"Ha. A car. I got a car." I told him all about the Escort, then asked how the play-reading committee had gone.

"We picked *The Odd Couple*. The one with girls. I volunteered you to be the stage manager."

The boy was almost to the corner of the next block. "Wait, stage manager?"

"Yeah," he said. "It's something we can do together. It'll be fun. It's okay that I volunteered you, right?"

"I just don't know if I'd be any good at it." I craned my neck to see the boy turn the corner at L Street and walk out of sight. "Anyway, I have to go. I was only supposed to drive around the block. My parents are taking me out to dinner."

"Mmkay. Call me later? After dinner?"

"Yeah."

"Happy birthday again."

I found myself driving down L, along Third, up M, zigzagging through the Avenues looking for the boy until my mom called wondering where I was and I headed back home.

We ate at our favorite Middle Eastern restaurant, where Mom and Alan discussed the likelihood that one of their tropical fish, Estella, had fin rot. Mom asked me about my day; I said it was fine, and told them about being sung to twice — first in homeroom by everyone, then at lunch by Gil. I listened to myself spin a story of birthday fun, crazy friends, and meaningful presents. The person whose day I was describing had not spent the majority of it fighting a sense of impending doom.

Mom gave me an envelope with two hundred dollars in it. "I was thinking clothes," she said. "You've kept yourself in such good shape, honey, you never dress that body of yours to show it off a little."

"Mom . . ." She knew I hated to talk about the way I used to look, especially in front of anyone else, even Alan.

"Sorry, sorry," she said, waving her hands. "Anyway, never mind clothes, because now you'll need all of that for gas money."

Alan snorted. "We might need to take out a second mortgage for gas money."

They drank wine, held hands. I didn't eat much. Mom's comment, even though it had been a compliment, had put the Jennifer Harris cloud back over my head. I stared out the restaurant window at the street.

"Looking for someone?" Alan asked at one point, picking an olive off my plate.

I shook my head. "I was thinking about going over to Katy's. . . ."

"You should," Mom said, nodding. "Take the car. Go crazy."

"It's a school night."

"It's your birthday."

"I'm just saying. You made the rule." I pushed my plate away. "Maybe I will, though."

I knew I wouldn't, knew that the whole idea of me and Katy and Steph and a wild night out was part of the story I'd made up and told my parents about the birthday girl and her fun day at school.

The truth was we'd go home and I'd sit in my room and do my homework and try not to think too much about the past, and go to bed hoping to feel more like myself — or, I should say, more like Jenna Vaughn — in the morning.

There was something in our mailbox when we got home. I saw it as we pulled up and the headlights skimmed over the porch for a second — the very edge of a white envelope visible against the black metal of the box. Neither Mom nor Alan noticed; they were talking about making baklava and whether or not it was okay to use almonds instead of walnuts. A note from Ethan, I told myself, or maybe something extra from Katy or Steph for my birthday.

Except I knew, even then, that it wasn't any of those things. Not that I knew what it *was*. But in more than three years of having the friends I did, there had never been a note in my mailbox. Text messages, yes. Or e-mails. Not letters in envelopes on porches. Which is why I didn't say anything about it as I went in the house with Mom and Alan. See, this is what I mean about me and my birthday. Any normal person would have been excited, grabbed the envelope, and ripped it open expecting to find something good. Not me. I sat there imagining all the bad or scary things it could be. It could have been something from my biological father, who I only knew as Don Harris and had not seen since age three. It could have been from someone who had known me as Jennifer Harris — Matt Bradshaw, maybe — reminding me who I really was and that I wasn't going to get away with this Jenna Vaughn business for much longer.

Stalling, I got out my phone to call Ethan but ended up dialing Steph's number instead.

"Hey," I said, sitting on my bed. "I got a car."

"Yes! It's about time. When are you picking me up? Where are we going?"

"You sound like my mom."

"Really, Jenna, it *is* your birthday," Steph said. "Aren't you at least going to go surprise Ethan or something?"

"I have too much homework." Steph kept talking while I thought about the envelope. Maybe it was something for my parents. Maybe it had nothing to do with me.

". . . reigning Miss Predictability," Steph said, "proudly representing the fine state of Utah."

"My inability to be spontaneous is part of my charm."

"It's true. You wouldn't be you otherwise."

"Katy said . . ." I stopped myself, and reached across my bed to close the window curtains.

"Katy said what?"

"That I didn't seem like myself today."

"Katy says a lot of things you needn't pay attention to." She paused. "You *were* a little out of it, though."

I wasn't sure what to say. The fact that I hadn't hidden myself as well as I thought made me nervous. But then, having friends who noticed when I acted out of the ordinary — that was good, right?

"J.V.?" Steph said. "Still there?"

"Yeah. Birthdays are stressful for me," I said. "That's all."

"Why? You get presents!"

29

"This one time . . ." I swallowed, hardly able to believe that I was considering telling.

"One sec, potential hookup calling . . ."

Maybe I'd just say, *I had a bad birthday once.* I could say that I was at a friend's house, and his dad was mean and yelled at us. That was enough of an explanation, really, and it might help to say even that much.

"I'm back," Steph said. "I told him I was in the middle of something and I'd call him later. Which I won't, then he'll call me and I'll pretend I forgot, and —"

"Have you ever thought about just . . . being *honest?*" I was one to talk

She laughed. "Oh, Jenna. How little you understand. Anyway, you were saying?"

The moment, if there ever really was one, had gone. "Nothing. Just that birthdays involve a lot of attention and I'm glad it's over."

"In Jenna's world, Attention Bad. I forgot." Her call-waiting clicked in again. "Ooh, I want to take this one. Go do your homework. See you tomorrow."

"See you."

I went out of my room, through the dark kitchen, and stood quietly where I could see into the living room. Mom and Alan were watching a nature show. They were on the couch, Mom's feet in Alan's lap, his hand absentmindedly petting her toes. I had an impulse to join them, to wedge myself in there and feel Alan on one side of me and Mom on the other and the TV in front of us and the solid wall of the house behind us. I'd like to fall asleep like that, hemmed in, and wake up and have a better day in front of me.

Then Mom sat up and kissed Alan and I felt like a spy, and also a little grossed out, so I went back through the kitchen, through the front room, and, finally, out the door and into the cold dark. Our porch light had been out for weeks, giving the yard and the walkway an eerie sort of feeling, like anyone could be out there, watching. I pulled the envelope out of the mailbox quickly, stuck it in the pocket of my jeans, and went back to my room.

Jennifer Harris.

Is what it said on the envelope. Not Jenna Vaughn or J.V., like my friends sometimes called me. Jennifer Harris, a person I had not been for more than four years. How could whoever it was have found me with my new name? It's not like I'd sent a change of address to Jordana Bennett and Matt Bradshaw. The printing was neat, precise, the envelope a little lumpy like there was something in it.

Even before I opened it, my mind was already racing ahead, gathering facts and retrieving memories and putting together bits of information into what I suddenly realized was the truth. It was like when you see a movie, a mystery, and you make assumptions based on what you see until the very end when you get one piece of information that makes you realize that everything you thought, everything you assumed, was wrong, and you wonder how you ever could have believed what you did. And the truth I came to as I opened the envelope was this: Cameron Quick was not dead. Or I should say, I had no proof that he *was* dead, and I never had.

I had Matt Bradshaw and Jordana Bennett — just kids, kids who hated me — telling me a story.

I had a mother saying *I'm sorry,* comforting me, then encouraging me to move on.

My most convincing evidence was that I'd never heard anything from or about Cameron again, and I believed he would have contacted me if there was any way he could, but he hadn't.

Until now. I knew it as I ripped open the envelope, my heart stretching.

The card had an abstract art sort of picture on it, painted in sweeping strokes of blue and gray and purple like a movie sunset. When I opened it and saw what was inside, my palms tingled. A note to a dead person, from a dead person. Still holding the card, I ran to the front door, outside, down the walk. Where was he? I jogged up to the corner, looking up and down the street, but there was no one. I stopped at the top of the hill, looking down at the lights of the valley, knowing he was out there somewhere.

When I came back in the house, Mom called from the family room, "Jenna? Everything okay?"

"Yeah. Fine."

I wasn't fine. I lay on my bed and looked at the card over and over and over again. When Ethan rang my cell, I didn't answer. What I wanted to do was cry — with happiness, sorrow, confusion, fear. But it all gathered in my throat and stuck. I sat up and opened the curtain so I could look out my bedroom window, as if I might see him hiding there in the dark, looking at me with his big eyes, seeing me the way I hadn't been seen since he left — the real me who was still there under the layers of my new unfat body and acceptably stylish clothes, my nice house, my nice stepfather, my new car. I stared at the card forever, opening and closing it, trying to believe what I was seeing:

Happy Birthday, Jennifer

And a pencil-line drawing of a house. And under a piece of Scotch tape a ring, just a cheap ring with a blue glass stone.

I'm back, it read.

Love,

Cameron Quick

CHAPTER 4

ETHAN PICKED ME UP THE NEXT MORNING, SINCE WE HADN'T discussed how we'd alter our routine now that I had my own car. Regarding Cameron, I'd decided that the best thing was to go forward with my regular life until I knew more. The best thing was to keep on being Jenna Vaughn; stay on the map, follow the plan. I'd tried my hardest not to look like I'd been awake most of the night, but still, Ethan did a double take when I got in his car.

"I know," I said. "I had trouble sleeping."

"You should have called me or IM'd. I was up until, like, one."

"I just . . . didn't feel well. Like maybe I ate something at the restaurant last night that wasn't entirely good for me."

"You said you were going to call me, though," he said. He got like that sometimes, not picking a fight or anything but wanting the last word or making sure everyone knew he was right.

"I know. I'm sorry." I stared out the window while we drove to school, looking at every male we passed and thinking it might be Cameron. Ethan didn't notice. He fiddled with the radio and told me about his ideas for *The Odd Couple* and how excited he was to be assistant director.

I'd almost told Alan about Cameron that morning. As soon as I heard him up and making coffee, I went to the kitchen to get a cup. Something about the early hour and Alan looking so harmless in his checkered robe made me feel like maybe I could say it. I could tell him all about everything that happened. But then he'd tell Mom and I'd have a million questions to answer that I couldn't, and besides, I wasn't sure I was ready to tell anybody anything. Still, that was twice in a twenty-four hour period I'd come close to talking about things I never had — first with Steph, then Alan.

"We have five minutes till first bell," Ethan said, pulling into a corner of the student lot. "Wanna make out?" He wiggled his eyebrows at me. What could I say? *Not really. No thanks.* Instead I leaned into him and we kissed. He pulled back a little to slip his hand up my shirt and then stopped. "Your eyes are open." He laughed, looking over his shoulder in the approximate direction my eyes had been fixed while I watched kids go into the school building, so sure somehow that I'd see Cameron among them. "What are you looking at?" Ethan asked.

"Nothing."

"You never kiss with your eyes open."

I shrugged and straightened my shirt. "We're going to be late."

He leaned back in his seat and took a few deep breaths, then asked, "Are you sure you're okay?"

"Yeah. Just tired."

While he gathered up his backpack and coat, I reached into my sweater pocket and closed my fingers around the ring. My heart pounded.

"You coming?" Ethan asked from where he stood outside the car.

"I really don't feel so good," I said, suddenly afraid to move. If Cameron Quick was alive, what else was out there that I didn't know about? "Maybe you should take me home."

"I hope you're not *sick* sick, since you just transferred about a billion germs into my mouth."

Cootie girl, came a voice in my head, the kind of voice I hardly ever heard anymore. *You and your gross germy self . . . you're lucky anyone wants to kiss you at all.* "No, not like that. Just. I don't know. Not good."

"You'll feel better in a couple hours, I bet," he said. "Anyway, we have a test in physiology, remember?"

"I know." We heard the first bell ring. I got out of the car and hoisted my backpack onto my shoulder. "You're probably right. I'll probably feel better soon."

I was a zombie all morning. When anyone asked what was wrong, I used the "I'm tired" excuse and changed the subject. I watched the door of every classroom waiting for Cameron to walk through. At lunch, I sat where I could see both cafeteria entrances, while Steph and Katy and Gil and Freshman Dave and Ethan all talked about the play. Freshman Dave asked Steph if she was going to try out for the lead.

"There are two leads," Katy said. "Both for girls. That's the beauty of it." She turned to me. "What about you, J.V.? There are some small parts, you know."

"She's stage manager," Ethan said through a mouthful of cafeteria spaghetti. "She doesn't like to be onstage."

Steph watched me from across the table. "Since 'she' is sitting right here, maybe 'she' could speak for herself. Just an idea." Steph was not one to put up with anything and kept the boys in line.

I chewed my dry sandwich, wishing for a nice big chocolate shake to wash it down. Ethan's thigh nudged mine. I guessed I was supposed to say something. "Oh. No, it's okay. He's right. I don't want a part," I said. "Stage manager is fine. It's great."

Steph rolled her eyes. "I'm so convinced."

They might have said more after that, I don't know, because right then I noticed Ethan's car keys in the unzipped outside pocket of his backpack. He was talking to Gil and Katy, the three of them reliving something funny that had happened during the junior year play. When he jumped up from the table to act out part of the story, I slid my hand into his backpack, pulled out the keys, and hid them in my lap before he turned back around. Stealing was easy. I'd had lots of practice as Jennifer Harris, who needed a steady supply of snacks to get through the day. Sometimes that meant taking from stores, other kids, even Mrs. Jameson's desk drawer once when she let me stay after school to help organize the reading corner.

This time it was all for a higher purpose, not just to stuff my face. I needed to get out of there and *do* something, *find* him. Sitting and waiting for something to happen was the worst kind of torture.

Steph saw me. I knew it when her eyes met mine with a

questioning sort of look. Then Ethan's story was over and he was sitting again and Steph opened her mouth. I looked down, expecting to hear something like, "Ethan, did you know Jenna just jacked your keys?" But what she said was, "We haven't had a movie night since school started. When can everyone come over? My dad just put in surround sound for the flat-panel."

I got up to throw my trash away and slipped the keys into my sweater pocket. When I returned to the table, I collected the rest of my stuff. "I left something in my locker . . . have to get it before fifth."

Steph stood. "I'll come with you." She ran her hands through her hair while Freshman Dave watched, mesmerized. "If that's okay." I couldn't exactly make a scene about it, so I said sure, she could come, and thought quickly about what I'd tell her when she asked why I'd swiped Ethan's keys.

"I want to take his car to get washed and detailed." I sorted stuff from my locker into my backpack — what I needed for homework, what I could leave. "As a surprise."

"Nuh-uh. Jenna Vaughn would not cut class to do that. I know you."

I faced her. "Sure about that?"

Her eyebrows went up and her lips curled into a smile. "Sex? Sex! You're taking his car to run home, spread flower petals all over your bed, and chill the champagne. You're finally giving it up. Today. Right after school. Does he know? Let me help set it up. Please please please."

"Steph." I closed my locker and started down the hall. "Sorry to disappoint you, but that's not it. I just have to do something."

"Something you don't want Ethan to know," she said, following me. "Something that's worth ruining your flawless attendance record for. Come on, Jenna, let me in on it. I don't want to go to class, either. We'll have an adventure! We haven't had one in a long time. Not since flamingo flocking sophomore year . . ."

I stopped walking. The postlunch hall crowd was starting to thicken, as much as any crowd could thicken at Jones, and I wanted to get out of there. Alone. But I also didn't want Steph to get mad and blab to Ethan. And . . . I was about to cry. In public. Which was something I strictly *did not do* anymore. "This isn't like that," I said, my voice starting to wobble. *Crybaby.* Just hearing the name in my head was enough to keep the tears from coming. "This is something serious. I don't even . . ."

"Okay. It's okay. Come on." Steph took me by the elbow and led me down the main stairs, out the building, to the student lot. Before I knew it, she and I were both sitting in Ethan's car. "Let's go," she said. "You can trust me. I promise."

In a brief moment of good sense, we ended up driving to my house to get my car, then I followed Steph in Ethan's back to the school lot, where we left it parked in the exact same space it had been in. "What about the keys?" I asked as Steph got into the Escort.

"I put them on the ground, right behind the front tire. He'll figure he dropped them this morning."

I looked anxiously toward his car. "What if he doesn't find them? What if someone else finds them first?"

"Relax, Jenna. What will be will be." She rolled down the window and draped her arm out as we drove away from the school. It was warmer than the day before by at least ten degrees. "So. Where are we going?"

"I don't know." We got onto North Temple and headed away from town. I hadn't thought this far ahead, and definitely hadn't thought about having someone else with me. Being in motion and out of school made me feel marginally better, though now I gnawed on my cuticles as I drove slowly, scanning the streets for anyone who might be Cameron. This was difficult, given that the picture I had of him in my mind was frozen in childhood: the big eyes, an often-worn striped T-shirt, a Norman Rockwell swoop of dark hair. I almost ran a red light, slamming on the brakes hard enough that Steph had to put her arms on the dashboard to steady herself.

She swore. "If you tell me what we're looking for," she said, "I could do the looking and *you* could keep your eyes on the road."

"Who," I said.

"What?"

"Not what, who."

"Who what?" Steph put her hands to her temples. "Okay, stop. This isn't a comedy routine. Speak in complete sentences."

"We're looking for a who, not a what." My cell chimed with the text message tone. I had Steph reach in my coat pocket to check it.

"It's Ethan. He wants to know where we are." Her phone chimed next. "And there he is again. Doesn't like you out his sight, does he? Should I answer?"

We passed a bus stop where a cluster of people waited, including a tall, youngish guy with dark hair. I pulled over and got out. Steph leaned out her window. "Jenna? Where are you going? Should I answer or what?" I got within a few feet of the tall guy and saw he was too old to be Cameron. I got back in the car and felt Steph's eyes on me as we kept driving down the street.

"Tell him I have cramps," I said. "And a headache."

"Oh, good one." She texted Ethan and flipped her phone shut with a snap. "I told him not to worry — I'm taking care of you. Not that it's any of his business. Now, *who* are we looking for?"

The closer we got to the airport, the more deserted the streets were except for little bunches of people at bus stops. I wasn't going to find Cameron Quick here. "A ghost," I said, turning the car around.

"You're not going to tell me." It was tempting. Steph was a decent candidate, being the kind of girl who always had plenty of secrets of her own. I just wasn't sure she could keep mine. Also, how could I explain Cameron Quick without also explaining Jennifer Harris and everything that came with her? "Well?" Steph asked.

"I guess I'm not."

She didn't press. "You're suddenly very mysterious, Jenna Vaughn."

• • •

After dropping off Steph, I drove around a while longer, still looking, until I found myself parked in front of the 7-Eleven on K Street. I went in and walked up and down the aisles with my coat over one arm. It had been a long time since I'd done what I was about to do, but the feeling was as familiar as ever: desperate and inevitable, like taking Ethan's keys earlier had just been a warm-up. My fingers rested on a cheerful orange package of peanut butter cups and then on a Kit Kat bar, before finally closing around a Milky Way, neat and compact, just like I knew it would be. I drew it under my coat, stopped to read the magazine covers, and walked out of the store.

CHAPTER 5

I POSITIONED MYSELF ON THE COUCH WITH A FLEECE BLANKET over my legs and the heating pad resting on my stomach. A cup of tea sat steaming on the coffee table to complete the illusion of me having cramps and a headache. My excuse for cutting class would at least look legitimate if Mom got home demanding to know why she'd been paged at work by the school office. Except it turned out that she had to work overtime and Alan was the first one home, so I'd gone to all that trouble for nothing. He was far easier to convince, especially when it came to anything that fell under the category of "female trouble."

"Hey there," he said, standing by the TV. "Your mom got a message from the school that you weren't in your last couple of classes. Everything all right?"

I rattled a bottle of Midol at him, knowing that would end all questions.

"Oh." He went over to the fish tank and peered through the glass. "Well, next time answer your phone when we call to find out what's up, okay?"

"Okay. Sorry." I closed my eyes and listened to Alan go through his postwork routine: check on the fish, sort the mail, take off his shoes and tie, inspect the fridge and cupboard in search of a snack.

"You want food?" he called. "I can fix us some dinner."

My stomach was already beyond full from the tuna sandwich and leftover spaghetti I'd wolfed down along with the stolen candy bar, but I was still hungry in the back of my throat, in my chest, in my limbs — every part of me but my stomach. "Yeah," I said, "dinner would be nice."

"It's not too cold out to fire up the grill. Or I can just wimp out and do mac and cheese. . . ."

I could already picture Alan's hand reaching back into the cupboard for the shiny blue box, and the way the butter would melt into the orangey powder. "That sounds good. Mac and cheese." I'd be good tomorrow, I told myself. I just had to get the eating out of my system and then I could get back on track.

Later that night, after Mom and Alan had gone to bed and the house was quiet and I couldn't sleep, I sat out on the porch in my pajamas and robe, pushing against the cement with my slippered feet, back and forth in the aluminum rocker. We'd had a rocking chair, Mom and me, in our old apartment, before Alan. It was my favorite place to sit with a book and a snack and the comforting motion. Now, I thought about Ethan and how I owed him a phone call or at least an e-mail, but every time I imagined what I would say I came up empty. Even my many years' experience of faking my way through life wasn't helping; I'd been brought to a complete stop by the idea of Cameron being alive, and Jennifer Harris being alive right along with him. As if she had ever died. Believing that was my mistake; I realized it the second I'd slipped that candy bar under my jacket, as easy and natural as if I'd never stopped.

There on the porch I thought I heard something, and suddenly held still. The *swish-swish* sound of the rocker halted and everything became strangely sharp, vivid: the cold night breeze that blew through my hair, the sound of leaves scraping along the walk, the shadow of the trees against the blue-black sky.

Where *was* he?

"Cameron," I whispered. "Cameron Quick. Come home."

I waited, as if he'd just appear out of the dark. He didn't. So I conjured him up, circa 1998, because I knew this memory hadn't died any more than Jennifer had.

He's standing behind his father, with something in his hands. The thing in his hands is greeny brown and drooping. It's Moe, his lizard. It doesn't move.

Cam says it's your birthday. He made you something. Yeah, that's right, but I wouldn't get too excited, I mean, don't get your hopes up. I've seen it and it's pretty much a piece of crap.

I look at Cameron and try to tell him with my eyes that it's okay; whatever he made is going to be good and I'll like it because he made it. That's a lot to try to say with your eyes and I don't know if he understands, so I find my voice. *I'll like it,* I tell Cameron, but his dad thinks I'm talking to him.

Sure, you say that now, but the proof is in the pudding, right, so let's take a look. He turns toward Cameron's room and then stops and looks back, right at me. *Well come on already, I'm not going to send an engraved invitation.*

After one last glance at the front door, I follow them toward Cameron's room. Cameron goes first, moving fast, Moe's tail hanging over his arm. His dad wears boots, the kind you hike in, and he walks in long-legged strides like he's going to step on Cameron's heels. And then there is me, my pink sneakers on the gray carpet, hoping that we'll just look at the gift and his dad won't say anything else about me being chubby or Cameron being stupid, and Moe is only sleeping, not dead, and then I can go home.

CHAPTER 6

ON FRIDAY, I DROVE MYSELF TO SCHOOL AND FOUND ETHAN
waiting for me at my locker. Seeing him there in his favorite cargo
pants and the red high-tops, and the smile he gave me as I walked
toward him, I wanted to throw my arms around him and be reminded of who I was. But then two very cute and tiny freshman girls
passed him and looked over their shoulders, and then at me, and
whispered something and laughed and I thought, *They know.* Even
they could see it wasn't right for someone like me to have a boyfriend like him.

"Feeling better?" Ethan asked, slinging his arm around my neck.
The move was nothing unusual but seemed a little invasive, and I felt
bloated and undeserving. Without thinking about how it would
make Ethan feel, I backed away. He let his arm drop, looking hurt.
"Apparently not."

"Sorry," I said, trying to sound it. "Hormones."

"Okay."

We walked to homeroom without saying anything. He went off

to talk to Gil before the bell rang and I sat in my seat, finishing trig homework and chewing my gum, hard. I'd skipped breakfast to make up for my binge and all I could think about was a chocolate croissant I'd had over the summer from the Avenues Bakery. My mind was totally absorbed by the idea of buttery and chocolatey when Katy hurried in, fell into the seat next to me, and whispered, "Who's the new guy?"

I lifted my head and focused.

He was in the front row, his back to us in an untucked plaid flannel shirt. We stared at the back of his dark head, Katy craning her neck. "I can't see his face. But I predict cuteness. You can tell even from the back." She folded her hands and bowed her head in mock prayer: "Please, God, let this one stay."

"Cameron." I barely said it. It was more like a thought accompanied by lips moving and a little air coming out.

"Huh?" Katy asked. When I didn't answer, she looked at me. "Are you okay? Your face just turned all pasty."

"Cameron," I said again, louder. He heard me and turned his head. His big eyes locked on mine and the rest of the room disappeared. There was no Katy, no Ethan or Gil, no Steph. No walls, no windows, no door. Maybe what was happening was a dream, a lucid dream you almost make happen by wanting something so much. But then the room and the other people in it shimmered back into existence and Mr. Moran was introducing the class to the seventeenth member of Jones Hall's senior class: Cameron Quick.

Katy sighed and slumped down into her seat. "Oh my hell," she muttered. "Those eyes."

"I'm sure I can count on all of you to make him feel right at home," Mr. Moran said, smiling out over the class.

"You know him," Katy said. "Tell me everything." We were on our way to physiology, hanging back from the rest of the group. She clutched at me, her eyes wide and neck turning pink the way it did when she was excited about something.

After homeroom Cameron had walked past me and handed me a note. All it said was, "I'll explain when we're alone." I wanted to hear his voice and touch him. It had been all I could do to keep from grabbing him right then to see if he was really real.

"I don't know him." My knees barely functioned, my mouth almost too dry to speak.

"You said his name, Jenna!"

"I think . . ."

Ethan, in front of us, turned back and reached out his hand for me to take. I jogged a little to catch up with him and took it, a direct physical link to the present. Katy stayed right in step. I continued, "I think he went to my school when we were kids. Like, little kids."

"And you recognized him? Just like that?"

"Photographic memory."

"Well, he's hot," she said, "and tall. Taller than me. Do you know how hard it is for me to find guys taller than me?"

"Yes," I said, which seemed insufficient. What snappy-but-not-mean comment would Jenna Vaughn come up with? "Based on our two thousand past conversations about it, I have a notion."

The explanation for all of this was probably simple. I'd been thinking it through since getting the birthday card: He'd moved away, was all, and fifth-graders weren't renowned for their skill at keeping in touch. Matt Bradshaw and Jordana used it to torment me, because they could. And now he was back, end of story.

But he hadn't said good-bye. He would have said good-bye.

And my mother had also believed he was dead, so . . .

"Are you saying you know that kid?" Ethan was asking. "That new kid?"

"Not really." I squeezed his hand, harder than I meant to.

"Ow." He pulled his hand away, shaking it.

"Sorry. Do we have a play meeting or anything after school? A rehearsal?" I wanted to force us all forward before we took too long a detour with questions about Cameron.

"We can't have a rehearsal until we have a cast, and we can't have a cast until we hold auditions."

"So, no?"

"Right," he said, giving me a sideways glance that I ignored.

I didn't see Cameron again until Steph, Katy, and I walked into the small cafeteria for lunch. Katy spotted him first, of course, standing near the back of the lunch line, holding a yellow plastic tray flat to his chest with his big hands. I couldn't get over how tall he was — six two, at least. At the same time he looked exactly like himself, exactly like I'd expect him to. We watched him while waiting at our usual table for Ethan and Gil and everyone else.

". . . the nice thing about him is," Katy was saying as she twirled a thick strand of red hair around her fingers, "he's not *too* cute. I mean, he's gorgeous, but he's so quiet, right? He could stay under the radar. Which would be good. The radar is my enemy."

Steph looked over at him. "No disputing his cuteness."

"How do you know he's quiet?" I asked Katy.

"Oh, he's quiet all right. Just look at him. He's *brooding*."

"He's not brooding. He's standing in line." I thought the exact words I'd said to Gretchen back in fifth grade: *You don't know anything about Cameron, so don't act like you do.*

"Go invite him to sit with us," Katy said, jabbing her finger into my arm. "Pretend you're walking by to get a drink or something and you just happen to notice him, and then you can be all, 'Oh! Cameron! I didn't see you there. Why don't you come meet my friends?'"

"That sounds so natural, Katy."

"Go ahead, J.V.," Steph said, watching me carefully. "Give little Katy here the first shot at the new boy. Anyway, no one should have to eat alone on his first day at Jones Hall. That's not what we're about."

"And *you* keep your hands off," Katy said to Steph, only half kidding. "Save one for me for a change."

I got up from the table, first, because I couldn't stand to hear Katy and Steph talk about him like he was the last piece of chicken in the bucket, and second, because I figured that if Cameron was going to be invited to our table, it would be better if I was the one to do it. "Okay." I tried to sound confident and casual, like talking to

Cameron was no big deal at all. "But I'm not going to create an elaborate ruse just to ask someone to sit with us. Because unlike Katy, I am normal."

Steph laughed. "If you say so."

He saw me approaching.

My steps slowed. Ethan and Gil had come in; I felt Ethan watching from the other side of the cafeteria.

Cameron kept his big eyes on me. My stomach twisted.

Keep walking, Jennifer, don't stop.

Then I was standing in front of him. His hair was dark as ever, darker. His eyebrows were thick. There was a little stubble on his chin. He was practically a man, but the person I saw was the boy, exactly as I remembered him. My knees gave way.

Watch out, everyone, Fattifer is going to faint.

This time, Cameron was there to reach out a hand and catch me, keep me from dropping right to the floor. "It's okay," he said, voice deep.

I nodded and swallowed hard. Now, my hand was on his forearm. He had on a long-sleeved shirt but I felt the warmth of him through it, the bones and muscle and blood and skin of a real, live person. The cafeteria line inched forward and I remembered where I was. I took my hand away, aware of Ethan and my friends watching. "You're not dead," I said.

"Not that I know of."

The girl in front of us had obviously stopped paying attention to her friends in order to eavesdrop. I lowered my voice. "When can we talk?"

"I can be at your house at four today," he said. It wasn't soon enough for me. I wanted to hear him talk for hours, not just to hear an explanation but to hear the little things in his voice that would remind me, give me more pieces of the puzzle.

"How did you know where I live?"

"I'll explain."

The girl tilted her head closer to listen in. Between that and imagining Ethan watching us, I began to talk louder, animated and friendly, so that I wouldn't look at all serious or meaningful. "You should sit with us. After you get your food, I mean, just come over to our table and you can meet all my friends, and, you know" — I took a breath — "eat your lunch."

He glanced over at our table, where Katy and Steph were waiting.

"If you want," I added. "You don't have to."

The line started to move again. We were holding things up. "It's all right," he said. "Tell them I had to go see the school office about my locker combination." He moved with the line and I went back to the table.

"Well?" Katy asked.

Steph watched me. "You okay, J.V.? For a second it looked like you tripped or something."

"Yeah. Um, he had plans."

"Already? I knew it," Katy said, slapping her hands on the table. "Stupid radar!"

CHAPTER 7

"WHERE ARE YOU GOING?" ETHAN HAD CAUGHT ME IN THE HALL
hurriedly shoving stuff into my backpack. The hours between
lunch and the end of school had been excruciating. I tried not to let
it show.

"Home . . . you know. Nothing exciting."

"You didn't even wait for me after class." He watched as I tore
and crumpled papers that were keeping my backpack from zipping.
"What's the rush?"

"My mom wants me to do some stuff around the house before
she gets home from work." I couldn't look into his eyes. I concentrated on his mouth, instead, which I hadn't kissed all day. "I'm sorry.
I can pick you up for school tomorrow if you want."

"Yeah, okay." He leaned into me and slipped his hand around
my waist, letting his fingers rest on the skin above my jeans. "When
can we be alone?"

The first time Ethan had done that — touched my skin that way
and talked to me low — I thought I'd pass out. We were at the
Gateway Mall, a week after I ran into him at the library over the

summer, just walking around and shopping when we stopped at the top level rail to watch people walk by below us. He put his arm around me, touching my skin with his warm fingers and talking close to my ear. *I like you, Jenna.* It was the first time a boy had ever touched me like that. It surprised me. We'd been friends from school but it wasn't like I'd been harboring a crush on him or anything. That day at the mall he touched me and I decided I was attracted to him and it was about time I had a boyfriend and just like that we were a couple. Sometimes I worried that I should be feeling more for him than I actually did, but I tended to push those worries aside and focus on how it felt to be part of it, to be seen by everyone as worthy of couplehood.

Now, I didn't feel much other than worry over the time and the need to be home so that I could pull myself together before four o'clock. But I kissed him as sincerely as I could and promised I'd call that night. When I headed toward the student lot, I sensed that he was still standing there, watching me walk away. I was in too much of a hurry to look back.

3:48

It wasn't a panic attack. I know this because I looked up "panic attack" online when I thought that's what I was having. Nor was it generalized, free-floating anxiety, which were also listed on the Web site. I *knew* why I felt the way I did. My heart pounded; I worried I would throw up. At 3:50, I went to the kitchen and let a spoonful of honey melt in my mouth. It coated my tongue and slid down my throat and momentarily calmed me.

3:54

The thing was this:

After that day at Cameron's house, because we'd never said anything about it, I sometimes wondered if it happened. I dreamed it, maybe, or made it up. Maybe my mom and all my teachers were right back then about my imagination and how it was very nice and important for children to have imaginations, but not when it kept them from living in the real world.

But I think I know the difference between things that happened and things I imagined happening.

This had happened, just like the ring and the walks home from school and the I Love You.

3:57

It was very possible that I should be worried. What did I really know about Cameron Quick, anyway? What Gretchen said about him growing up to be a school shooter popped into my head and I couldn't let it go. Here was this guy I hadn't seen in eight years who tracked me down and knew where I lived and turned up at my school for no good reason. Like a stalker.

4:02

I remembered:

The fall before he went away, we were walking home from school and took a detour. There was an office park a few blocks from my apartment building. It was nice, for an office park, with man-made ponds and fountains and a stand of aspens between one of the buildings and the Jordan River Parkway. We wandered into the aspens and lay on the ground hoping for a breeze so that we could hear the leaves clatter — that's what aspen leaves do, they clatter.

The ground was cold against my back and at first I worried about bugs, but after a few minutes of lying there with neither of us speaking, the sound of cars on the nearby road faded out and the afternoon sun blazed behind the trees making green-gold light all around us. I turned my head so that I could see Cameron. His hand was inches from mine. I wanted to take it, or at least stretch my fingers out to see if they reached his. But we hadn't touched since the day at his house, with his father there watching, making it something it shouldn't have been. I pulled my hand closer in and looked back at the sky and the quaking leaves.

4:09

I watched from the living room window as he came up the walk. The impossibility of it struck me again — that he would be back, that he would find me and show up in my life. But there he was, all six-plus feet of him in the jeans and shirt he'd worn earlier, taking long steps toward the house. I moved to the door and resumed my watching through the peephole. He stopped on the first of the three stairs up to our porch and stared at our house. I imagined that he could see through the walls, like a superhero, see me on the other side of the door, and then through me, through my skin and into my heart, which he would see was afraid.

Who would he expect me to be?

He stood so long on the bottom step that I worried he was going to change his mind and turn around, and before I really knew what I was doing I opened the door.

"Hi."

"Hello."

"Do you want to come in?"

He walked up one more step and shook his head. I went toward him. We were the same height now, him on the second step and me on the porch, and I could see right into his eyes. "Maybe we can sit out here," he said.

"Okay." I lowered myself into the aluminum rocker, slowly. I had this feeling that if I moved too fast, or touched him, he'd disappear. He finally came all the way onto the porch and sat in a plastic chair a few feet from me. "Hi," I said again.

"Hi."

"You're here." I studied his profile. It was so exactly how I remembered it — the way he always had his head tilted slightly down, looking out at the world as if from underneath something. "Sorry," I said, "for staring."

"Go ahead and stare. I don't mind."

"You look different," I said, "but also the same. It's weird."

"You, too."

He stared back at me for so long that I wanted to look away. Instead, I closed my eyes, trying to make a picture of little Cameron materialize. I saw him in that striped T-shirt and his jean shorts, skinny legs and falling-down socks. Him sitting across from me in Mr. Lloyd's office during speech therapy, squinting with effort every time he got to a word with an r in it. I remembered the way he'd look at me when he got it right, shy and proud, a Cameron Quick that no one else at school ever got to see. And the time he handed me a half-squished Fig Newton, still warm from his palm, at lunch. I had more memories of him than I thought, and they were coming at me quickly now, too fast to really hold on to.

Cameron, big Cameron, said, "Are you there?"

I smiled, keeping my eyes shut. "I'm staring at you in my head now."

"Where are we?"

"Mr. Lloyd's."

"Your hair is in two braids."

"Crooked braids," I said. "My mom was always in a hurry."

I sat still and held the picture in my mind, as real as when I'd lived it. Big Cameron breathed next to me, his own eyes closed for all I knew. Or maybe not, maybe still looking at me. And beyond that, the sound of leaves on cement every time a breeze fluttered by. Still farther, cars passing a few streets away.

And I turned the image in my mind around so that instead of facing Cameron, I was looking at myself: Jennifer Harris, braided hair and secondhand clothes and missing teeth and baby fat. She would leave Mr. Lloyd's office and end up home alone, in an empty apartment, standing in the middle of the room with her backpack at her feet. It seemed like she — I — had lived an entire lifetime on that green, threadbare couch, equidistant from the TV and the refrigerator.

She looked back at me with two questions: *How could you have left me?* And *Why didn't you say good-bye?*

I assumed they were questions for Cameron. I opened my eyes, ready to ask, but knew that if I even attempted to say those words the tears would start. Instead I asked, "How did you find me?"

"I've followed you for a long time." He must have mistaken the look on my face for alarm or fear, and said, "Not literally. I just mean I never lost track."

But it wasn't fear, or anything like that. It was an instant of realization I'd have a lot in the coming days: I'd been thinking of him as coming back from the dead, but the fact was he'd been there all along. He'd been alive when I cried in my room over him being gone. He'd been alive when I started a new school without him, the day I made my first friend at Jones Hall, the time I ran into Ethan at the library. Cameron Quick and I had existed simultaneously on the planet during all of those moments. It didn't seem possible that we could have been leading separate lives, not after everything we'd been through together.

"... then I looked you up online," he was saying, "and found your mom's wedding announcement from before you changed your name. I didn't even need to do that. It's easy to find someone you never lost."

I struggled to understand what he was saying. "You mean . . . you could have written to me, or seen me, sooner?"

"I wanted to. Almost did, a bunch of times."

"Why didn't you? I wish you had." And I did, I wished it so much, imagined how it would have been to know all those years that he was there, thinking of me.

"Things seemed different for you," he said, matter-of-fact. "Better. I could tell that from the bits of information I found . . . like an interview with the parents who were putting their kids in your school when it first started. Or an article about that essay contest you won a couple years ago."

"You knew about that?"

He nodded. "That one had a picture. I could see just from looking at you that you had a good thing going. Didn't need me coming along and messing it up."

"Don't say that," I said quickly. Then: "You were never part of what I wanted to forget."

"Nice of you to say, but I know it's not true."

I knew what he was thinking, could see that he'd been carrying around the same burden all those years as me.

"You didn't do anything wrong." It was getting cold on the porch, and late, and the looming topic scared me. I got up. "Let's go in. I can make coffee or hot chocolate or something?"

"I have to go."

"No! Already?" I didn't want to let him out of my sight.

"Don't worry," he said. "Just have to go to work. I'll be around."

"Give me your number. I'll call you."

"I don't have a phone right now."

"Find me at school," I said, "or anytime. Eat lunch with us tomorrow." He didn't answer. "Really," I continued, "you should meet my friends and stuff."

"You have a boyfriend," he finally said. "I saw you guys holding hands."

I nodded. "Ethan."

"For how long?"

"Three months, almost." I couldn't picture Cameron Quick dating anyone, though he must have at some point. If I'd found Ethan, I was sure Cameron had some Ashley or Becca or Caitlin along the way. I didn't ask. "He's nice," I added. "He's . . ." I don't know what I'd planned to say, but whatever it was it seemed insignificant so I finished that sentence with a shrug.

"You lost your lisp."

And about twenty-five pounds, I thought. "I guess speech therapy worked for both of us."

He smiled. "I always liked that, you know. Your lisp. It was . . . you." He started down the porch steps. "See you tomorrow, okay?"

"Yeah," I said, unable to take my eyes off of him. "Tomorrow."

I stayed up late IM-ing, at first just with Ethan, about an English assignment and auditions for *The Odd Couple* and what we were going to do that weekend — everything but what was really on my mind. Talking to him was the last thing I wanted to do. What I wanted was to go over and over the conversation with Cameron, remember every detail of his voice and the way he cleared his throat and how his eyelashes were long and soft over his big eyes. I wanted to think about how I was going to break the news to my mom.

Mom! Mom! Guess what? Cameron Quick is alive!

No.

Because he was never dead. I'd been thinking about this. If I was a mom and my daughter came home and told me that her only friend — who'd recently moved away, which was hard enough — died in a freak accident, I'd do some checking. I'd do some asking around. I'd make sure she got to send flowers to the funeral or something, had the chance to talk about it and remember him. Instead she gave me two days off of school and told me to move on and make new friends. I knew she was busy back then, but I couldn't believe she was too busy to have done a better job helping me deal with it.

Anyway, my immediate problem was Ethan, and since I'd been on a bad mini streak of neglect and lying, I needed to put all the other stuff aside and give him some attention. While I chatted with him, Steph came online and we started chatting in a separate window.

Steph: It's him, right? The WHO we were looking   for yesterday. It's that new guy.

Me: Hold on.

Ethan typed away; I contributed smiley faces and LOLs and OMGs as necessary, while figuring out what to tell Steph.

Steph: You know Katy is already obsessed, right?

Me: Yeah.

Ethan: Come over Saturday night. My parents have a work thing. House to OURSELVES!

Me: ☺

Steph: So what's the deal? You don't have to tell me. Okay, you have to tell me.

Ethan: Is that a yes????

Me: I think so. I have to ask my mom.

Steph: Maybe I can help. You need someone to talk to. Just tell me!

Ethan: We can order pizza. Pizza and a movie and who knows what else?!

Steph: Hello?

She was right; I needed someone to talk to. It wasn't going to be Katy, and it most definitely was not going to be Ethan.

Me: He came over today.

Ethan: Who?

I jerked my hands off the keyboard, realizing I'd accidentally posted to the wrong window.

Ethan: Who came over?

My fingers hovered. I knew I had to type something fast or it would only look worse.

Ethan: Jenna??

Me: Cameron Quick. The new kid? He stopped by to say hi.

I'm not sure why I told him that, other than that I couldn't think up a lie quickly enough.

Steph: Are you there?

I ignored her and held my breath waiting for Ethan's reply. IM fighting is the worst, because you can't see the other person's face or hear any breathing like on the phone — nothing. Ethan could have been momentarily interrupted by a parent or he could be sitting there hating me and it would all look the same on my screen.

Me: It was no big deal. He just wanted to see my new house. I didn't know he was coming.

Ethan: You didn't know? Then how did HE know where you LIVE?

Good question. I thought fast. Ethan didn't know anything about my history. He didn't know I thought Cameron was dead. He really didn't know anything about me. As far as he was concerned, my life had started in ninth grade, when I walked into Jones Hall and promised myself I would smile, I would look nice, I would make friends.

Me: His mom and my mom are friends. They stayed in touch, I guess.

Ethan: Oh. His mom was WITH him? Today? Why didn't you say so??

I started to correct him and tell him no, Cameron hadn't come with his mom. Then I backspaced over everything and started over.

Me: Because I'm dumb? ☺

Ethan: You're not DUMB. Dummy. ☺

We chatted a little more; Steph signed off after I hadn't answered her. By the time I got up from the computer, my breathing had returned to normal after the stress of lying to Ethan, but I ended up in the dark kitchen anyway opening the fridge as quietly as I could so as not to wake up Mom or Alan. I needed sweet, I needed creamy. There was no pudding, no yogurt, nothing for making chocolate milk, no ice cream, not even any applesauce. All I found was part of an old bag of chocolate chips in the freezer. I dumped them into a bowl and heated them in the microwave until they started to melt. I got a spoon, went back to my room.

I sat with my back against the door. The curve of the chocolate-coated spoon fit exactly right against my tongue.

Sometimes I missed being Jennifer Harris. Obviously, being Jenna Vaughn was more of an overall advantage in life, but there were moments I missed being Jennifer the way you can miss versions of yourself when you get a totally new haircut, or a favorite pair of jeans finally wears out. Even though it was sad that I'd spent so much time home alone eating and reading, the truth was that those were some of my favorite memories. Getting lost in a book with something sweet or salty or hopefully both, like stacks of crackers with butter and jelly, seemed, in some ways, the closest I'd gotten to complete and total happiness.

The two questions came into my head again: *How could you have left me? Why didn't you say good-bye?*

I missed myself the way I missed what Cameron and I had before that day at his house, and how time almost stopped when we were together. We didn't have to explain it or understand it or talk about it, ever. Everything was innocent. It just was. Nothing, nothing could be as simple as that ever again.

CHAPTER 8

CAMERON'S PRESENT IS A DOLLHOUSE. IT IS RIGHT IN THE middle of his bedroom and made out of wood. It's not fancy like a Barbie Dream House. It doesn't have furniture or anything, just a wooden back and two wooden sides and a slanty roof and it's open in the front. The side walls have little windows that are almost square but you can tell Cameron did it by hand, with a tiny saw, maybe. Because they are a little bit crooked.

He looks at me, still holding limp Moe in his arms. *It was too big to bring to school,* he says.

It has two stories inside and comes to my waist. I can picture how I'll put Rufus and Bitty, my toy mice, inside. I run my finger along the inside edge of one of the windows. Anything that could make a splinter has been sanded away.

You made it?

He nods.

Cameron's father laughs. *Okay, okay. It's the worst dollhouse you've ever seen in your life, right? Just tell him. He knows.*

No, I say. *It's good.*

Me saying that the dollhouse is good makes something change in Cameron's father. Now he's looking back and forth at us in a way that makes me wish I hadn't said it. But if I hadn't said it then Cameron might think his dad was right, which he wasn't. So I don't know what I should have said.

If you like it so much, why don't you play with it now?

It's confusing the way he talks. I wouldn't mind playing with the dollhouse, but Cameron doesn't move.

His father studies me and scratches at his dark mustache. *I thought he was sweet on you but now . . . now I'm not so sure. I think maybe he just wants someone to play dolls and hopscotch and dress-up with. Yeah, that makes more sense, now that I take a good look at you. You're not really the type to be anyone's girlfriend, are you?*

This lines up with the kind of thing I hear people say about me at school and I wonder what is wrong with me that even Cameron's father can look at me and see the truth: that I'm ugly and fat and no one wants to be my friend. It makes me feel guilty. The fact that Cameron does want to be my friend somehow makes his dad act mean like this. If I were thinner and prettier, if I had the right clothes like Jordana and Charity, then maybe it would make Cameron's dad see him in a different way. A better way.

I think I have to go home, I say. Not so much to Cameron's father but to Cameron himself, who is just standing there next to the dollhouse, his eyes big but his lips clamped shut.

When I was Cam's age I had games I liked to play with my little girl-

friends, too. But it sure as hell wasn't hopscotch and dollies. We played house. We played doctor. That's what normal kids do.

His father is leaning against the door, getting comfortable, and his face lights up the way my mom's does when she has a good idea about what to fix for dinner.

Maybe you just don't know how, huh?

CHAPTER 9

IT'S AMAZING HOW ADAPTABLE WE ARE; HUMANS, I MEAN. LESS than twenty-four hours after seeing Cameron again for the first time in eight years, back from what I'd believed was the dead, I'd already adjusted to the new reality. When he walked across the cafeteria to our table, the sight of him seemed almost ordinary. Almost. Because while the sight of Cameron now seemed ordinary, the fact that I was sitting at a table full of social non-pariahs, including a boyfriend who was mine, was what seemed wrong.

Watching Cameron come toward us I could see why Katy used the words "hot" and "gorgeous" to describe him — he definitely had nice hair and a long, lean body with broad shoulders, and the eyes. I wondered what Jordana would think now if she saw him. He set his tray on the end of the table, not particularly near any of us.

"Everyone," I said, "this is Cameron Quick."

Ethan stood to reach over the table and shake his hand. "Hey. I'm Ethan."

"We were . . . we both went to the same elementary school," I said, even though they'd heard that basic explanation already, "and then he moved, and . . . now he's moved back, so he's here. Here he is."

Steph looked at me like she knew I needed help, and said, "I'm Steph, this is Katy." Katy smiled and waved; Steph pointed down the table, "Gil, Freshman Dave, Junior Dave, and obviously Jenna."

Cameron finally spoke, mostly to his lunch tray, "Hi. Nice to meet you all." I watched him to see if he sneaked any looks at Steph, like most guys did when they first met her, dazzled and intimidated by her starlet body and model face. He barely seemed to notice.

Ethan took a bite of his burrito. "So you and Jenna were in the same class when you were kids?"

Cameron glanced at me. "Basically."

"What was Jenna like back then?" Gil asked. "Got pictures?"

Cameron smiled. "Don't need pictures. I got her up here," he said, tapping his forehead. I groaned, making a joke of it, while inside I worried over what he would say. He might tell them I was fat, or about my lisp or my thrift-store clothes or how much I'd changed. "Two braids. Sweet eyes. Good heart. Adorable. Just like she is now."

Gil looked at Ethan.

Katy studied her apple, eyebrows raised.

Steph said, "Jenna has all that and more, except maybe the braids. Which is why everyone loves her. I dare you to find one person in this school who does not like Jenna Vaughn." Based on the color of Katy's neck, I think there might have been *one* person who didn't like me, at least for the moment. "So, Cameron," Steph continued, "auditions for the school play are next week. You should come. We need more males of the species to try out."

"Not my thing," Cameron said.

"Okay, so you don't want to be onstage. You could be backstage."

"With Jenna," Gil said helpfully. "She's the stage manager —"

Ethan talked over Gil. "But if it's not your thing," he said, "it's not your thing. You don't even have to *have* a thing if you don't want."

"Right," Katy said, "no thing required."

Cameron didn't respond, didn't even act like anyone was waiting for him to say anything. He just ate his lunch, scooping spaghetti onto a piece of bread and folding the bread over into a sort of sandwich before putting it in his mouth. I was fascinated by the most mundane little details of him — how he held his paper napkin in his left hand while he ate with his right, the space he took up when both his elbows were on the table.

I was suddenly aware that I'd been staring at him, and everyone else at the table was staring at me. They were all done with their lunches. I wondered how much time had passed.

"Um," Katy said to me, "are you all right?"

Steph caught my eye and smiled slowly.

"Oh, yeah." I concentrated on my half sandwich trying to think of something witty to say, but I was in total Jennifer Harris territory now, spacing out and forgetting how to make simple conversation.

Cameron picked up his empty tray. "Nice to meet you all. See you later." He lifted a finger toward me. "Bye, Jennifer."

We watched him leave, then Gil said, "How come he calls you Jennifer?"

I crumpled up my lunch bag. "Because that used to be my name."

"Really?" Ethan said. "I didn't know that."

"I changed it a long time ago."

"He's shy," Steph said, still watching the spot where Cameron had been sitting.

Katy smirked. "Not with Jenna."

Ethan surprised me by coming to Cameron's defense. "That's because they've known each other forever. I'd be nervous, too, if I were meeting all you retards for the first time."

"Good point," Junior Dave said.

I drove Ethan home after school even though what I wanted was to talk with Cameron for a hundred more hours. We sat in front of his house — his family had a bungalow near the park, a small brick thing that barely held him and his parents and his two little sisters, Carly and Hannah. He took my hand and wiggled my fingers one by one. "You look nice today."

"I do?" Hard to believe, as lumpy and tired and out of sorts as I felt.

"Yeah." He got closer, played with my earring. "Your hair is all . . . wavy."

"Thanks for being so nice to Cameron." I don't know why I said that right then, totally ruining the mood Ethan was obviously trying to get me in. But talking, flirting, having a normal conversation about our usual things felt impossible. He stopped playing with my earring and leaned back.

"Sure. I mean, I've got nothing against the guy."

"Exactly," I said, nodding.

"As long as he stays away from you, he can be my best friend if he wants." He took my hand again. "Why don't you come in? No one's home for a while."

This time it was me who pulled back. "He knows I have a boyfriend. We can still be friends, though," I said, resisting the urge to tack a "right?" on the end of my sentence.

"Well, yeah. Within reason."

"What does that mean?"

"It means 'within reason.'" He turned away from me and stared out the windshield. "Jenna, think about it. If there was some hot girl who'd known me half my life and described me as having 'sweet eyes' and being 'adorable' and she suddenly turned up out of nowhere, how would you feel?" He made air quotes while he talked, and even imitated Cameron's deep voice in a way that didn't sound entirely complimentary.

"You're friends with Steph," I said. "That doesn't bother me." Which, actually, was not totally true. But I would never, ever let on that it bothered me, because no one likes an insecure, possessive girlfriend. No one likes an insecure, possessive boyfriend, either, a fact that Ethan did not seem to grasp.

"So you're saying you're going to be hanging out with Cameron?" he asked.

"I'm saying he's my friend."

"I'm saying you're my girlfriend."

"I'm saying I *know* that, and you have nothing to worry about."

He sighed. "Why don't you just come in?" He made puppy dog

74

eyes at me and I said yes and we went straight to his room and closed the door. He needed reassurance. I needed reassurance. Which was probably why we ended up breaking our firmly established makeout boundaries in a big pile of Ethan-smelling blankets on his bed, with his cat, Milhouse, curled up near the pillows.

The kind of feeling I got from being with Ethan that way was something like when I ate, the same private sort of comfort that I got when I had my favorite foods all to myself. It didn't seem quite right that it would feel like that. Because being with someone was supposed to be about intimacy and trust along with feeling good. The point was sharing something with the other person, making this special connection you weren't making with someone else. That's what my mom always said, anyway. Mostly, though, I went inside myself while I experienced it all — his hands on me and mine on him, his mouth, the warm climby floating, the intensity and release. I stayed utterly silent through it all, eyes shut, concentrating and not wanting it to ever be over and at the same time wanting it done. It was not unlike the way I always wanted food to last forever while also being anxious for it to be gone so that I could breathe again and go on with my life.

Afterward I curled into a ball alongside Ethan with my forehead on his chest. He pulled me close. "Was that okay?" he whispered.

I nodded against him.

"Are you sure? We kind of bent the rules, and . . . Well, I don't want it to be like you felt like you had to or something."

"Ethan, I wanted to," I muttered. "It was good."

"Okay." He tucked the blankets around my shoulders. Milhouse stretched and jumped off the bed. "Because you seemed kind of, I don't know. Far away."

I thought about that, and what I should say back that wouldn't make Ethan feel bad or make me sound weird, but then we heard the garage door go up and scrambled to realign all our clothes and arrange ourselves in a convincing configuration of textbooks and school binders. By the time his mom poked her head in his room, we were calmly discussing *The Old Man and the Sea* with the door open.

"Hi guys, I'm home." She scanned the room, as if looking for evidence of something. Fortunately Ethan never made his bed so it didn't look any more or less disheveled than usual. "Are you saying for dinner, Jenna?"

"No, thanks, Mrs. Green," I said, closing the book I'd just opened, as if exhausted from an hour of studying. "I actually have to get home."

Ethan walked me out to my car. "I didn't mean to be an ass," he said, holding the door while I climbed in the driver's seat. "About Cameron, I mean."

"I know."

"Just . . . you know. I think he likes you."

I laughed it off. "No, he doesn't. Not like that." Ethan couldn't possibly understand it, what Cameron and I meant to each other and how different it was from anything like romance or a crush. "Pick me up tomorrow?"

"Tomorrow is Saturday, silly. But you're coming over tomorrow night, remember?" He glanced toward the house. "My parents are leaving at six, then Carly and Hannah are getting picked up at six-thirty, so you could come at seven or something?"

"Okay," I said. He bent down to give me a slow, sweet kiss, and I drove off.

The farther away I got from Ethan's house, the more I felt lost. I wanted to go back and see him again, or drive by Steph's, or even call Katy. The things that made up my life as Jenna Vaughn seemed slippery and uncertain. I didn't go back to Ethan's, though, because I thought it would seem weird or needy, and really it wasn't Ethan per se that I wanted, more the idea of him and the fact of us being a couple. I didn't drive by Steph's because I could tell she sensed something about me and Cameron I wasn't ready to tell her. And I didn't call Katy because I knew she'd only want to talk about how to get Cameron to like her.

Mom and Alan couldn't make me feel unlost, either. I was almost certain now that Mom never really believed Cameron was dead. She was smart, she was a nurse, and she knew what he meant to me. If she'd believed the story about Cameron she would have found out more and talked to me about it. I knew she'd lied, but I didn't know how to ask for the truth.

Right as I was thinking these things, I drove by Smith's. I circled the block and pulled into the lot. I stayed parked for a few minutes, trying to talk myself out of what I was about to do, but soon the automatic doors were swishing open and I checked out the situation. The store was crowded with moms doing predinner shopping, and lots of their loud kids running around. I was just one of a dozen people in the candy aisle and it was easy to take the bag of mini chocolate bars and let it drop quietly into the gym bag I'd brought in, unzipped. Knowing it was there in my bag gave me some satisfaction, but anxiety about whether it would be enough and whether it would be the right kind of enough kept me walking up and down aisles until a bag of corn chips and a pint of cookie dough ice cream also ended up in my bag.

An employee walked by with some go-backs for the freezer and I imagined him looking at my open bag and my lack of any grocery cart or basket, so I moved down the aisle and tried to act like a regular shopper: frozen peas, a diet meal, some veggie burgers. I actually bought those things in the express lane. I had the money. I could have paid for the other stuff, too, but I didn't.

CHAPTER 10

I HAVE TO GO HOME.

That is what I tell Cameron's dad. I want Cameron to say something, but he is staring down at Moe.

Put that back in the cage, Cam, his dad says. _We'll deal with it later._

"That" and "it" is Moe. Cameron takes three steps to the cage in the corner of the room, lifts the top, and sets Moe down gently. For a long minute he stares into the cage, not turning around. I keep my eyes on the back of Cameron's head. Outside, more leaves fall by the window and I think how we could be outside, crunching them under our feet in the cool air instead of in this small, hot room that has one too many people in it.

The first thing you need when you're playing doctor is to decide who's gonna be the doctor and who's gonna be the patient.

Cam turns around, finally, to see what his father will say next.

When I was a kid the boy was always the doctor. His father looks at me. _But they've got all kinds of lady doctors these days so it could go_ *either way. And frankly I don't know if Cam has the nuts or the smarts to be the doctor, so it looks like you're up.*

I have to go home, I say again. This time I turn my body toward the door and take a step, then another, and another. Cameron's father reaches his long arm in front of me and the door closes with a hollow click, leaving the three of us together in the tiny room.

Midnight. After Mom and Alan went to bed, I put on my pajamas and got the ice cream and a spoon and the bag of mini candy bars. I started out with my back against the door again, but once a small pile of wrappers accumulated next to me I worried that one of my parents could wake up and come to my room for some reason, and it would be hard to clear away the wrappers without being caught. So I moved myself and everything else into my bedroom closet, with the door open enough so that light came in and I could see as much as I needed to.

At first, I'd hold a candy bar in my mouth until it warmed up enough to start softening, then I'd take a spoonful of ice cream, which would make the chocolate hard again, just for a few seconds, until it all began to melt together. Then I'd take some ice cream and balance a candy bar on top of the spoon and put it all in my mouth at once and chew, even when the cold hurt my teeth, pressing my tongue into the bits of cookie dough to taste for the mix of salty and sweet.

But it wasn't working.

The memories of that day at Cameron's house wouldn't stop. I told myself that it was useless thinking, since I couldn't change anything now. I couldn't go back in time and make it unhappen. I told myself it was okay, that I'd grown up into a regular person and had a normal, productive teenage life. I told myself that worse things had happened to other kids — much, much worse things that you could hear about every single week if you just watched the news.

I worked at getting different Cameron memories in my head, better ones — the day in the aspen grove, the note in my lunch box — but they wouldn't stick. All I wanted was to talk to him. Without a phone number or e-mail or an address that I knew, he was as unreachable as he'd been the last eight years.

I closed the closet door with my foot and finished the ice cream.

CHAPTER 11

I WOKE EARLY SATURDAY, FEELING LIKE CRAP — HEADACHE,
nausea, intense thirst. I promised myself I'd be very, very good for
the rest of the weekend and got up for a glass of water. Alan's laptop
was open on the kitchen table but he wasn't there. I wanted to see
his crooked, comforting face. I found him standing at the fish tank,
in the bleach-spotted blue sweatpants my mom pretended to hate,
his curly hair matted to the back of his head from sleep.

"What's the prognosis?" I asked. "On the fin rot, I mean."

He turned, a little startled. "Oh, hi. I think Estella is okay. But now
I'm worried about Monty. Does he look lethargic to you?"

I studied the little pink-and-black platy hovering near the bottom
of the tank. "I don't know. Maybe he's not awake yet."

Alan sprinkled some food over the water. We watched as fish
darted up to the surface to eat. "And what are you doing up?" he
asked. "Trouble sleeping?"

"Kind of." I checked the tank's aerator. The living room was dim
and the house was quiet and I knew Mom would probably be asleep

for another hour. It seemed like I could say things then and there and maybe not have them be as real as they would be if I said them when the sun was all the way up. "This . . . kid I used to know in grade school started at Jones Hall this week. We were, like, pretty good friends." Monty swam across the tank to catch a flake of food that had been slowly sinking. "There he goes."

"I didn't know . . . you . . . had any friends from back then," Alan said carefully.

I rested a finger on the cool glass of the tank, considering what to say, what to not say. "Just this one boy."

"Ah. A boy."

"In fact, yes," I said, turning away from the tank and toward the kitchen. "Is there coffee?"

"Of course." He followed me into the kitchen and we both got a cup. I sat at the table and watched him. There was something about his bare feet on the kitchen floor I liked: his big crooked toes with gray and brown hairs sproinging all around, the knobby ankles sticking out from his too-short sweatpant legs. I kept my eyes on his feet as he tuned in NPR on the radio, toasted his English muffin, and covered it with peanut butter.

"How's the car running?" he asked.

"Great. I think I've only put twenty miles on it. The horn doesn't work, though."

"I'll take a look. Probably just a fuse." Alan settled in front of his computer, chewing his English muffin and sipping his coffee. "So tell me about this friend, this boy."

"Well," I started, and then wondered if Mom had told him about Cameron Quick. Maybe Alan already knew more than I did. "It's complicated," I finally said. "How's the writing?"

"Oh, that. I've abandoned the poems for the time being. I do have this idea for a screenplay, though." Alan, a creative writing hobbyist, proceeded to give me a rough outline of the story while I drank my coffee. My headache was starting to subside, and I tried to tune my brain in to the day before me: homework, chores, eating right, getting some exercise, Ethan. I figured I should probably touch base with Katy and/or Steph at some point. ". . . and finds the treasure on the ranch, *exactly* where his grandfather said it would be," Alan was saying. "So what do you think?"

"I like it," I said, nodding thoughtfully as if I'd been listening.

"Hm." He rubbed his beard. "It sounds terrible to me."

"Don't overthink it. I'm going to get back in bed and do some reading for English."

"Good," he said. "Conserve your energy, because I think your mom has a lot of raking planned for us today."

Once in my room, I shut the door behind me and cleaned the wrappers and ice cream container and napkins out of my closet, putting them in two layers of plastic grocery-store bags and then shoving those into the bottom of my trash can. When that was done I made my bed and straightened my room and brushed my teeth and put on clean pajamas, and then I felt okay again, like the night before hadn't happened, like I was handling my life just fine.

• • •

We — Mom, Alan, and I — were out front doing the garden work when Cameron came walking up the hill. Mom saw him first. "I hope this kid isn't selling those coupon books," she said under her breath. "Say we already bought one."

"He's my friend," I said, wondering if she'd recognize him, if I could get away with giving him a fake name.

Alan stopped bagging leaves and rose slowly from his squatting position. His knees popped audibly. "Ow."

As Cameron got closer, I laid down my rake, straightened my hair, wished I'd put on some makeup. Mom had now stopped working, too, and lifted her hand to shield her eyes from the sun. "Do I know him?"

"Yes."

He was just a few yards from us now.

"Oh my God," Mom said. I tried to read her expression, but her hand still mostly covered her face.

"Hi," Cameron said to us all.

Mom looked at me, incredulous. "Jenna, why didn't you *tell* me?"

Alan extended his hand. "Alan Vaughn."

"It's Cameron Quick," Mom said to Alan before turning back to Cam. "You're Cameron Quick. Come here and let me hug you."

I watched them, Mom standing on her toes to reach around Cameron's neck, him bending low. I hoped for her to say something like, *We thought you were dead,* proving me wrong about her lying. Instead, she asked, "How is your mother?"

"Fine."

"Cameron goes to Jones Hall now," I said.

"You go to Jones Hall? Here in Salt Lake?"

"Just started Thursday," he said.

"I never thought . . ." Mom said, shaking her head. "Jenna, I can't believe you didn't say something."

They talked, and I waited for her to point out the obvious: that Cameron had been dead and now he was alive. But she never said it. They talked about Cameron's mother and his little brothers and sisters, which I'd somehow completely forgotten he had, but she never made one mention of his death. I glanced at Alan to see what he knew, if anything, but he was distracted with a lawn bag that wanted to blow away.

I almost said it: *Isn't it amazing? We thought he was dead, but here he is, right in our very own front yard!* When I opened my mouth, Cameron said to me, "I thought you might want to go get some lunch or something."

"Now?"

"Yeah." He looked at the piles of leaves. "I'll help you finish this first."

"Go ahead," Alan said, "we can handle it."

Mom smiled a strained kind of smile, her eyes never leaving Cameron. "Sure. Go on."

We ended up at Crown Burgers, across from each other in a small booth near a window.

"You didn't tell your mom about me," he said.

"I didn't have a chance."

"Okay." He took a bite of his burger and chewed slowly before saying, "What. Just say it." Two days and already he could read me better than any of my friends.

"Is it that obvious?"

"Can't hide anything from me. You know that."

"I'm just . . . confused. Because we thought you were dead. At least, *I* thought you were dead."

He laughed. "Dead? Why would you think that?"

"I heard at school," I said. "And I told my mom, and she didn't say that you weren't."

He was quiet; chewing, staring.

"And," I added, "why else wouldn't I have heard from you?"

"I came back."

"Eight years later!"

"You're mad at me," he said.

"No," I said, shaking my head. "I'm not."

"Yes you are. It's okay. I'd be mad, too."

"I'm not! I'm . . . not." I stabbed into my Greek salad with my plastic fork. "Anyway, never mind. You're not dead, you're here, I'm happy to see you and happy you're alive."

"Not that simple, though, is it."

I'd forgotten this about Cameron. How he didn't play games, never pretended, never just filled the quiet with meaningless words the way regular people did. If he opened his mouth to speak, it was to say something that mattered to him. That was part of why he never fit in. I used to be like that, too. Now I was a professional maker of small talk, filler of conversational space, avoider of awkwardness.

I was doing it even now, at Crown Burgers, too easily going from talking about Cam's alleged death to babbling about unimportant things like my problems in trig and auditions for *The Odd Couple.* "Hey, why aren't you in the drama class, anyway?" I asked. "Everyone has to take it." It was right there in the Jones Hall charter; the founders thought drama was important for our social development.

"They made an exception for me. I have too much catching up to do in real subjects."

I watched him eat, the way he followed every bite of a burger with exactly two fries and a sip of his drink. The curve of his fingers as he dipped into fry sauce, the shape of his lips around the straw — it was all information, all part of filling in the missing years.

"Do you want to help with the play?" I asked. "There's a lot to do even if you're not in it."

"If you want me to," he said.

"I do. I want you to. It will be fun," I said, trying to convince myself. "You can get to know everyone."

He appeared as unexcited as I felt at the prospect of him bonding with all my friends. "If you do something for me."

"Sure. What?" The way he looked at me, I knew that what he was going to ask was serious. Not like helping with a school play. "What?" I said again, quieter this time.

"We need to go back."

I put my fork down. "Where?" But I knew where.

"To all of it. The neighborhood, the school. My old house."

Our surroundings seemed to spin a little. I held the edge of the table for support. "That's why you came back."

"Partly."

"Is he . . . Do you still live with . . ." He shook his head. "Okay," I finally said. "All right."

"Tomorrow?"

"Tomorrow? As in the day after today?"

"That one."

The last thing I wanted to do was let him down, but when I thought about taking that trip back in time everything in me seized up. "I can't, Cameron," I said. "I need more time. It's only been a couple of days. Let me get used to the idea of you being alive, and then —"

"Nothing to be afraid of. I'll be there with you."

"I know, but . . ."

Something in his face closed, a door behind those eyes swinging shut. He looked at his watch. "Gotta be at work soon."

"Where do you work? Let me give you a ride."

"Don't worry about it. I'll get a bus."

And he left. I watched him walk out — he didn't say good-bye, he didn't even look back.

It scared me, how easy it was for him to do that.

CHAPTER 12

THAT NIGHT, MOM AND ALAN COOKED DINNER, WE ALL SAT AND ate, Mom talked. She talked and talked about the garden, the fish, the wine they were drinking, errands she needed to get done over the weekend, the other nurses on her floor, whether or not the scalloped potatoes were an accurate facsimile of her mother's. She addressed every single possible topic except the obvious one: Cameron. Even Alan barely got a word in.

He and I loaded the dishwasher while Mom made her Saturday night call to her sister in Maine.

"You know what's funny?" I finally said to Alan, handing him a rinsed plate.

"No. What?"

"We all thought Cameron was dead."

He stood up straight and took another dish from me. "Oh?"

"Yeah. He died. I mean, in fifth grade, I heard he died. I was really upset. I fainted at school when I heard. Mom took off work and everything."

"Huh." He placed our glasses on the top rack and closed the dishwasher door. "When did you find out that he wasn't dead?"

"Tuesday night."

"You mean . . ."

"This past Tuesday night. My birthday. He left me a card in our mailbox." Alan scooped some decaf coffee beans into the grinder, his bushy eyebrows furrowed. I wiped the counter down with a paper towel and polished the faucet. "So it's kind of strange," I continued, "that Mom didn't seem surprised that Cameron is alive."

"Well. Hm."

"Yeah. Hm." I tossed the paper towel in the trash. "I'm going over to Ethan's."

Ethan set his mom's kitchen timer to make sure we got in an hour of homework before we did anything else. I didn't mention my lunch with Cameron, but I sat there thinking about it, and the more I thought about it the more it bothered me that Cameron had come to my house with no warning like I could simply drop everything and go to lunch with him. And it bothered me that I did, when I had so much homework to do. And what he asked me to do bothered me — to go back to the scene of . . . *everything.* Just like that. My day had been fine and on schedule until he walked up and disrupted things and told me he wanted me to go back and relive everything. My *life* had been fine and on schedule until he left that card in our mailbox.

He didn't have any idea the steps I'd taken, the enormous mountain I'd climbed just to be able to do something as small as I'd done the second week of freshman year: standing next to Steph in the cafeteria line and saying, "So what are you going to get? The pizza looks okay." And how much it had required of me to say yes when she invited me to sit at her table that day rather than pre-reject myself for friendship the way I'd done ever since Cameron left me. He didn't know what a triumph it was for me to go one day without thinking of myself as Fattifer, to sleep through one night without imagining his father's boots on the carpet. And now, to ask me to go back through it all at a moment's notice, and to be upset that I couldn't say, "Oh, yes, I'd love to," well, maybe he was right. I was mad.

". . . auditions are Monday," Ethan was saying while he doodled in his notebook, resting his head on his other hand. "You have to be there, too, so you can start taking stage-managery notes."

"Aren't you supposed to be writing a history essay right now?"

He gently bopped my knuckles with his pen. "Yes, Mommy." He'd been sucking on cinnamon candy while we studied; his lips were ruby red. I leaned across the table to kiss them and sat back down. "There are still twelve minutes left on the timer," I said.

"Tease."

It was a nice scene — me and my boyfriend studying on a Saturday night. Except I wasn't really there. Narration ran through my head: There is Jenna Vaughn kissing her boyfriend, there is Jenna Vaughn with her trig book open, there is Jenna Vaughn smiling and playing footsie and acting like she is exactly where she wants to be.

What brings two people together, anyway? Maybe it was just convenience and coincidence that Ethan and I were a couple. Maybe if it had been another girl at the library that day, she'd be with him now at the kitchen table.

I looked at Ethan, wondering if I loved him at all.

"What?" he asked.

Then the timer buzzed, and Ethan smiled, slammed his book shut, took my hands, and led me to the bedroom. I followed, pushing all thoughts of Cameron and my mom out of my head. When we sank into the warm, dark pile of blankets and I went even deeper into myself, far away, exactly where I wanted to be.

CHAPTER 13

I STAYED IN MY ROOM THROUGH BREAKFAST, SITTING AT MY computer, even though I could smell bacon cooking and hear the waffle iron beeping and fresh coffee being ground. My mom had been asleep when I got home from Ethan's and I didn't know if Alan had talked to her or what, and all I really wanted was to stop thinking about Cameron and his dad and Ethan and everything else for one day, *one* day, and get my homework done.

Steph came online, her avatar in pajamas.

Me: What are you doing up? It's not even noon.

Steph: I know. I haven't been to sleep yet.

Me: Have your parents ever heard of "rules"?

Steph: No. Lucky for me. So what's the latest with your little friend?

Me: ?

Steph: Cameron. What's the deal. You thought I was gonna forget?

Me: No.

Steph: Katy wants him.

Well, she's not going to have him, I thought.

Me: I know.

Steph: Let's make it happen. Unless . . .

Me: Unless?

Steph: Unless.

Me: Are you typing in invisible ink?

Steph: You know what I mean, hon. UNLESS you don't want Katy to have him. For some reason.

Me: Such as?

Steph: Such as if YOU want him.

Me: I have Ethan.

Steph: You're not married to him. Think about it. I'm going to bed.

By noon I had to come out of my room to go to the bathroom and get coffee and food. Mom sat at the kitchen table, opening mail and paying bills. She glanced at me when I walked in and said, "There you are. I wondered when you were going to join the living. There's still coffee."

I said nothing.

She held up a piece of junk mail. "Are you interested in improving your life through Scientology?"

"Um, no."

She tossed it in the to-be-recycled pile.

"Where's Alan?" I asked, pouring coffee.

"Pet store, home store, grocery store . . . the usual Sunday rounds." Good Mormons didn't shop on Sundays, so it was Alan's favorite time to take care of errands without battling crowds. "What's your homework situation? I was thinking we could go to a movie, just you and me."

I considered it. We could sit through a movie together and then, trapped with me in the car, she'd have to answer all my questions. "Have you talked to Alan today?"

She twisted in her kitchen chair, one arm slung over the back. "Well, yes, of course I've talked to Alan today. I am married to the man." He hadn't said anything, obviously. Either my mom was truly clueless and had forgotten about the whole "Cameron is dead" incident, or she was intentionally hiding something. Neither scenario gave me a lot of confidence about how to proceed.

I opened the fridge and stared in, as if I'd find the answers there. I felt the memory of myself standing next to me, sticky hands on the door, looking for something to keep her company: maybe slices of bologna rolled into neat pink tubes and dipped in mayonnaise; sugar cubes; ramen with hot dogs; chocolate chips mashed into peanut butter and honey — anything and everything that was available in our small kitchenette.

I closed the door and turned to my mother. "Why did you tell me Cameron Quick died?"

She flinched but didn't say anything.

"Mom?"

"I didn't tell you that. You heard it at school."

"You let me believe it. You said he'd gone to a better place."

She pulled the chair next to her out from the kitchen table. "Come here, honey."

"No, just tell me."

"Jenna, there were things . . ." Her voice was quiet. "Let's just say, things you didn't know, and didn't need to know. It was a very complicated situation."

"So you knew. You knew he wasn't dead, and when I asked you if it was true, you *lied* to me."

"I didn't lie."

"Yes, you did! Do you think I *forgot* that conversation, Mom? Did you have any *idea* what Cameron meant to me? He was my only friend!"

She nodded. "I know."

"But you let me believe he was dead."

She put her hands to her head and closed her eyes. "I never thought we'd have to have this conversation. I never thought you'd see him again." She opened her eyes. "When I saw him walking up the street yesterday, I . . . Jenna, honey, you think *we* had problems? There were things going on in the Quick house that would make your blood curdle."

Things going on in the Quick house.

Things she knew about.

And things I knew about.

But we never told each other.

She continued: "Why do you think I never let you go over to Cameron's?"

"I don't *know*, Mom," my voice had started to shake, and I wasn't hungry any more, just sick to my stomach. "I was a kid, not a mind reader."

"Please come sit down, Jenna, really."

"I don't want to sit down."

She got up and came to me. "You remember that he moved a couple of months before you heard he died."

"Yes."

"I knew you were devastated when he moved. I knew school was hard for you. If I could have afforded it, I would have taken you out. Put you in private or homeschooled you, even, if I had the time." She touched my arm. "You were so sad those months, honey. It was awful to see. I'd started to ask around nursing school about a counselor or therapist for you, or if any of the girls at Village Inn had kids your age you could play with."

I pulled my arm away. "You could have fixed all that by telling me the truth, that he wasn't dead."

"Once I heard that you believed he was dead I thought maybe that would be easier for you to understand than the truth about what had happened."

"Which was?"

"Okay." Her voice turned matter-of-fact, recounting details as if for a police report. "Lara — Cameron's mom — and I met at a PTA thing one year. We were probably the only non-Mormon moms there that night, and we bonded. I should call her, now that she's back. . . . Well, anyway, I'd been listening to her problems, advising her. I don't know if you remember, but Cameron stayed with us once for a week while Lara was trying to work out different living arrangements. She had all the kids farmed out to the homes of various school friends."

"Of *course* I remember him staying with us, Mom. Do you think my memory is that bad? I was nine, not three. It was a highlight of my life." And suddenly I had another piece of that memory, as if the act of saying I remembered brought it back: My mom had made chocolate chip pancakes for Cameron and me one morning and we sat side by side at the counter in our kitchenette, watching cartoons while Mom brought us pancake after pancake after pancake, and Cameron got the giggles from his sugar high and I'd never seen him laugh that much, for so long.

". . . and when she came to pick him up," Mom was saying, still in her just-the-facts voice, "she told me that she had a plan. She'd made arrangements with a shelter. They were making room for her, and if one day she and the kids just disappeared, not to worry, and also not to tell anyone where they'd gone."

I stared at her. Ever since the day I told her Cameron died and she basically told me to get over it and move on, I'd stopped going to her for things other than the practical — food, clothing, shelter, homework help, basic companionship. It's not like we had a *bad* relationship, but whatever confidence I had in my mother's ability to be a mother had been buried along with everything else. Everything between us for the past eight years could have been different if she'd simply told me the truth. And she had no idea.

"You thought it was better," I said, "to let me believe my best friend was *dead* than to tell me that?"

"Jenna, I knew Cameron wouldn't be able to write to you because of the shelter rules. I thought believing he was dead would help you . . . move on. I tried to make the best decision I could at the time. And look, honey," she said, back in her mom voice, "things did get better for you after he left. You were strangely close, you know, different from any two kids I've ever seen. His mom and I used to talk about that, how you were so wrapped up in each other. I worried about that. If he'd stayed all those years he might *still* be your only friend."

She could have been right, but I was in no mood for agreeing with her.

"That didn't give you the right to lie to me," I said. It was the perfect opportunity to tell her what had happened on my ninth birthday, that I'd had my own run-in with things going on in the Quick house. Something stopped me, again.

Mom sighed heavily and looked away. "I did what I thought was best."

I drove around that night after telling Mom and Alan I had to return a shirt at the Gateway. Ethan called and texted me a couple of times but I ignored him. My mind was circling obsessively around the new information about Cameron, and I wanted more — more memories like the pancakes, more truth about the past, more truth about me. I wanted to see Cameron, see what he remembered about the week at my house, make sure he wasn't really mad at me. I wanted to tell him I'd buy him a cell phone myself if that's what it took to make sure he couldn't just exit my life again with no strings attached. I watched for people on the street with his tall, forward-leaning silhouette. It was cold, though, and a Sunday night, and the streets were nearly empty.

I got yet another text from Ethan: "Where r u?"

Where I eventually found myself: in the Crown Burgers drive-through line, waiting to pay for my bacon cheeseburger and fries and fry sauce, which I would eat alone in my car in the dark parking lot, wondering where Cameron was and how I could reach him, how we could reach each other.

Cameron's dad points to the bed. *Climb on up, son. Don't be shy.*

Cameron doesn't move. I look at him and think about the words "playing doctor" and things that happen at school privately between children and the showmeyoursI'llshowyoumine games that happened in corners of the yard in first grade and his father is right, everyone does things. Except now we're a little old for it. And normally no grown-ups are watching. I'm not as stupid as his father thinks I am.

Out the window leaves are falling and falling and falling. Into their backyard. Which is right there, just on the other side of the wall of Cameron's room.

I turn to Cameron. *It's okay. Go ahead.*

His father laughs. *Well I thought so.*

I say to his father, *You have to leave the room.*

What?

You have to leave. Then we'll play. He stares at me. Cameron climbs onto the bed and lays himself out like a patient. He trusts me, I can tell. I go to stand close to the bed and place my hand on his chest. Through his shirt, through his skin, I feel his heart beating. I turn back to his father. *Leave.*

CHAPTER 14

"WHY DIDN'T YOU CALL ME BACK LAST NIGHT?" ETHAN ASKED
while I got what I needed out of my locker before homeroom Monday morning.

"My mom wanted to do family stuff," I said. "Quality time. Et cetera. She worked a lot last week and —"

"But even just a three-second IM, or something? I needed to talk to you about auditions and stuff."

Auditions. Homework. Lunchtime gossip and boyfriend maintenance. These were the things I had to readjust myself to after the weekend of matters that seemed entirely separate and more real than any of this Monday-through-Friday living.

I asked Ethan: "When are the auditions, again?"

"Today! God, Jenna. I told you. You're coming, right?"

I closed my locker. "Right." I could barely see Ethan's eyes through his floppy hair, but the bottom half of his face looked hurt, irritated. And I felt bad, because he was right, I should have called him back. It would have been better than stuffing my face in the Crown

Burgers lot. I put my arms around him until he finally lifted his to hug me back. "I'll be there," I said.

Cameron didn't come to school, a fact that was simultaneously a relief and a disappointment. Without him there, maybe I could go back to being who I was, the person I'd successfully been just the week before. I went through the day trying to bring my total Jenna Vaughn–ness.

In homeroom, I volunteered to be in charge of senior announcements for the rest of the quarter.

During physiology, I conducted a small-group review of the nervous system.

In American government, I paid complete attention to the video on economics.

At lunch, I sat quietly next to Ethan and resisted any urge I had to look around the cafeteria in case Cameron had come late. A small non-Cameron-related drama erupted at the lunch table when Katy found out that she and Steph were trying out for the same part in *The Odd Couple*.

"Wait wait wait," Katy screeched. "I'm going for Olive! You knew that! You're supposed to be Felicia!" Her neck, unsurprisingly, went red.

"You never stated the part you wanted," Steph said calmly.

"It's obvious, isn't it? Me: slob. You: obsessive neat freak."

"Maybe I don't want to go for obvious parts anymore." Steph stayed stone-cold unflappable. "Mr. Bingry said I should stretch myself."

Katy slapped her hands on the table, sounding like she could cry. "Well, that's just great. I might as well get used to the idea of playing Girl on Street with Umbrella or whatever." She looked at me, pleading. "It's not fair. Tell her, Jenna."

Traditionally it was my job to keep Katy and Steph in line when these little fights came up, which they did on a semiregular basis. But I'd been thinking about Cameron and where he could be, and also what my mom said about maybe it being for the best that I believed he'd died. In a parallel universe in which Cameron and I continued on the way we were, right up through high school, what would my life be like now?

". . . Jenna? Are you there? Come in, Jenna." Katy was waiting for a reply.

"Steph should be able to try out for any part she wants," I said. "So should you."

"Right," Steph said to Katy. "I don't mind competing against you."

"What makes either of you think the lead parts are a sure thing?" Gil asked. "Maybe some sophomore will come in and blow Bingry away and you'll both be stuck working on props."

"Yeah," Ethan said. "It's called hubris."

"Bingry wouldn't do that," Katy said. "Seniors get the best parts. We've earned it."

"Why don't you try out for both parts, Katy?" I suggested.

"Fine, I will. Excuse me." She picked up her lunch and moved to a table of her tennis friends.

Junior Dave shook his head. "She won't."

They all went on to talk about past evidence of Katy's insecurity and cowardice. I obediently ate my low-fat, low-cal, low-carb lunch. "Steph," I said, looking down the table, "let's go to the gym after school."

Ethan looked at me in disbelief. "Um, auditions? The ones we were *just talking about?*"

"Oh. Yeah. After that, then?"

"Sure," said Steph, eyeing me curiously.

Twenty-seven kids turned out for the auditions: twenty-two girls and five boys. I sat at the back of the portable and watched while Ethan and Bingry called people in to read from the script. Junior Dave had been right about Katy — she didn't even read for Olive, instead going for a small part.

"So, when is the cast list going to be posted?" she asked after her reading.

"Probably by Wednesday afternoon," Ethan said. "Thursday at the latest."

She sighed. "Not that it matters."

I waved at her as she walked out, giving her a thumbs-up to let her know she'd done a good job. This wasn't so hard, I thought, this whole being a good friend and good girlfriend thing. I was even half looking at my trig while the auditions went on.

Mr. Bingry leaned outside to call in the next person, and Cameron walked in behind him, finding my eyes and locking onto them.

I soaked him up — in the day and a half since I'd seen him last, I'd already started to forget the details of how he looked.

I couldn't see Ethan's face, but his voice sounded overly cheerful when he said, "Hey, hi. Didn't see you in class today. That's cool. What part are you reading for? There are only two male parts, so . . ."

"I don't want a part," Cameron said. "I told Jenna I'd help backstage. You need people for that stuff, right?"

"Absolutely," Bingry said, excited. He twisted in his chair and looked back at me. "Jenna's the stage manager, so she's your gal. Jenna, your first crew volunteer!"

Ethan asked, "Don't we usually offer crew to people who audition but don't get parts?"

"We can never have too much help," Bingry said. "Especially from someone with some height and muscle for hanging lights, building flats, putting up pipe and drape —"

"And I have my own tools," Cameron said.

"Fantastic. A perfect specimen. Give your contact info to Jenna and we'll let you know when we're ready to build."

Cameron walked over to me in long steps while Ethan watched, leaned on my desk — the fingers of his big hands spread wide — and gave me his phone number. "Just got a phone this morning," he said as I wrote it down, trying to appear efficient and disinterested. "Now you can call me. Anytime."

I nodded. "Thank you." He turned and walked out.

Ethan scribbled something in his notepad.

Bingry called in the next reader.

Steph started in on me at the gym.

"I heard Cameron volunteered to be on the stage crew," she said, pulling her hair back. We were in the locker room, getting ready to cardio funk.

"Wow, news travels fast."

"So that will be interesting."

I put my bag in a locker and closed the door. "How so?"

"Jenna. Stop playing dumb." She stalked off to the big mirror over the sinks. I followed and stared at the two of us. She looked incredible, with her spray-on tan and low-rise gym shorts and tank top, whereas I was a lump in faded black stretch capris and my extra-huge Utah Utes T-shirt.

"What's your point?" I washed my hands.

She laughed. "Anyone can see you've been a total head case since Cameron showed up. Don't let Ethan forget you're his girl-friend." She turned to me and grabbed about a yard of my T-shirt fabric. "Oh my hell, Jenna, you have a shape, you know. You should show it now and then. Ethan might appreciate that."

"Ethan is very familiar with my shape, thanks." I pulled my shirt back.

"How many boyfriends have you had, Jenna?"

"Counting Ethan? Let's see. One."

"How many boyfriends have I had?"

"We've all lost count, Steph."

"So take my advice," she said, resting her long, slim arms on my shoulders. "Cameron is all mysterious and tall and obviously into you, and Ethan will feel threatened any second now, if he doesn't already. Make sure he knows he has nothing to worry about. *If* you want to keep him, that is. If you'd rather have Cameron, fine, just don't drag it out. Trust me — that only makes things worse."

"Cameron isn't 'into me,'" I said, removing her arms from my shoulders. "It's more like . . . I don't know. It's hard to explain."

"Well, whatever you want to call it, there's something going on between the two of you. Everyone can feel it." She handed me a towel and picked up hers. We walked out of the locker room, Steph looking back at me over her shoulder. "And if you don't want Cameron, help Katy get him. It's the least you can do."

When I got home, Alan was sacked out on the couch with his laptop. I nudged him over and sat down. "Mom's still not home from work?"

"Shortage on the floor, too many patients, not enough nurses. The usual." I chugged from my water bottle. "Good workout?"

"I guess."

"She feels terrible, you know," he said, peering over the top of his screen.

"You have no idea, Alan. There's so much more to the story, stuff she doesn't . . ." I stood up to keep myself from saying anything else. "Forget it. I need to shower."

• • •

Leave? Cameron's dad laughs.

I make myself not look at the window. Is there a screen? I can't remember. My hand is still on Cameron's beating heart. He does not say a word.

Leave, I repeat.

He isn't laughing anymore. Now his arms are folded. *All right, then. Here I go.* He takes a step backward. Now he turns and puts his hand on the doorknob. *I'm leaving.* He is through the door. With one glance back, staring directly at me with hard eyes, *See me leaving?*

The door closes behind him.

I run to it and push the lock button in.

When I turn, Cameron is still on the bed, frozen. *Get up.* I see that the window does have a screen. *Scissors,* I say.

Finally he understands, gets up, and goes straight to his dresser drawer instead of his desk. What he comes up with are not scissors but a knife, a big one. I stare at it for a second wondering why he has a big knife in his room. I open the window. Cameron starts to cut the screen.

Hurry, I say. *Hurry.*

Cameron cuts the screen with the knife.

The doorknob wiggles. *You locked me out. I can't believe you locked me out. You know it would be easy for me to break this door down . . . just one good shove.* Cameron's father's voice is still big, almost like he's right in the room with us.

Cameron cuts. I pull. Then the knife slips and falls behind the bed. We look at each other and his dad pounds the door again. I take the window screen and pull as hard as I can. Pieces of wire poke into my hands, stinging me and drawing blood.

For the first time I start to cry. Because I know if we don't get out it's going to be bad. And then it's quiet on the other side of the door, which feels almost worse than the pounding. I keep pulling the screen even though my hands hurt so much. *I got it,* I say. There is a hole in the screen big enough for us to climb through.

You go first, he says. He helps me out and I land on the dirt. My ankle hurts, and so does my head, where a little bit of my hair got caught and pulled out. Cameron climbs through and lands next to me.

He takes my hand.

We run.

As my eight-years-later self, I stood under the shower and let the water stream over me. I could almost feel my hands still stinging from the window-screen wires. There should be scars, I thought, and lifted my hands to my face to examine them. There should be evidence. But the skin was its usual shade of pinky-beige; a couple of torn cuticles but nothing else. I was the one who got us out, me, scared little Jennifer Harris. The memory of how it felt to escape and Cameron himself were the only evidence I had.

• • •

I woke up after midnight, thinking I heard footsteps outside my window. It's not the kind of neighborhood where you should be hearing footsteps anywhere near your house after dark. Usually it ends up being a cat or raccoon, but you never know. I listened, ready to run into Mom and Alan's room if necessary, but heard nothing more and fell back asleep.

CHAPTER 15

"LAST CHANCE FOR COFFEE," ALAN SAID, POKING HIS HEAD into the bathroom while I finished up my morning routine.

"Save me a cup. I'll get it in a sec." My hair would not do anything I wanted it to. There were dark circles under my eyes and my skin looked dull and PMS-y. I had some hair pomade in my gym bag, which I'd left in the car. I scurried out into the chill.

When I put the key in the car door, I gasped. The passenger seat was tilted all the way back, Cameron's long legs stretching under the dashboard. With his jeans jacket tucked around his shoulders and eyes closed, he looked so much like his childhood self. I opened the door carefully and crouched next to him. "Cameron?" I said softly. "Cam?"

He opened his eyes, blinking at the morning sun. "Hi."

"What are you doing?"

"Sleeping in your car."

"I see that." I glanced back at the house. "Do you want to come in? And have some breakfast?"

He nodded and got out of the car. I led him up the walk, through the front door, and into the kitchen where Mom was making her lunch. She looked up, surprise only crossing her face for a second. "Well. Good morning, Cameron," she said. "I think there's a cup of coffee left if Jenna doesn't mind sharing."

"You can have it," I said to him. "I'll get some on the way to school."

"Thanks."

Mom got a mug down for him and pointed to the half-and-half. "I'm off," she said, putting her lunch stuff into a paper bag. "Nice to see you, Cameron. Tell your mom I'd love to catch up with her." She gave me a kiss. "Be good."

"I will." We hadn't had any follow-up conversations since Sunday and I knew she was waiting for me to give some sign that I wasn't mad. I kissed her back, which made her smile.

"When are you ever not good?" Cameron asked, after Mom had gone.

"She says that to me every morning. For her it's synonymous with 'good-bye.' How did you get into my car?"

"You left it unlocked."

"Oh." The more obvious question was *why* did he get into my car, but that could wait.

We heard the jingling of Alan's keys. He leaned into the kitchen. "Bye, Jenna." His eyebrows went up when he saw Cameron. "Oh, hi there."

"Hi," Cameron said.

"Good to see you again."

"You, too."

"Well," Alan said. A long, awkward pause followed, during which we all glanced at one another and smiled politely. "See you tonight, Jen?"

"See you." He left, and I turned to Cameron. "So."

"You didn't call me last night."

"Was I supposed to?"

He looked down. "Just figured now that you had my number . . . Kept my phone on all night, just in case." He laughed. "I started to worry that it didn't work. Actually went out to a pay phone to test it."

"You could have called me. The way you left me after lunch on Saturday, I figured . . ." I ended there and shrugged, not wanting to be mad at him or get into any kind of argument. "Anyway, after auditions I went to the gym with Steph, and I'm so behind in my homework it's not even funny." Of course I'd punched in his number about eighteen times without actually ever calling him. I wasn't sure what I'd say, and worried about how I'd feel if he didn't answer.

"I shouldn't have left like that on Saturday."

"Yeah, well." I waved my hands. "Don't worry about it. I have to finish getting ready. There's cereal and stuff . . . just make yourself at home."

"I saw him walking to school," I told Ethan, "and I pulled over and offered him a ride. Like I would for anyone I know."

It's not like I wanted to get into this lie-telling habit with Ethan, but I really couldn't see any possible way he would understand Cameron sleeping in my car. *I* didn't even understand it. And Cameron, on the ride to school, had not offered any explanation.

"Okay, so why were you late?" Ethan asked.

"I was slow getting ready this morning. It happens."

He didn't look at me or hold my hand or do anything else to reassure me as we walked down the hall to government. "It's your first detention ever, Jenna. And — what a coincidence — it comes on a day when you show up with Cameron?"

"Yes." We got to our room and I held Ethan's arm to keep him from going in. For a second, I wondered why I was trying to stop him. I wasn't feeling liked or understood or even tolerated by him. But then maybe that was my fault, a result of all the lying and hiding and being someone I wasn't. Feeling desperate, I played Steph's card, even though it was a total fantasy. "I'm trying to get him and Katy together. I want him to hang out with us so that he can be around her and warm up to the idea."

Ethan snorted. "What makes you think he's going to go for Katy?"

"Opposites attract?" The warning bell rang.

Cameron came up to us, like he was waiting to go into the classroom. We were sort of blocking the door. "Excuse me," he said.

Ethan swept hair out of his eyes, jutted out his chin. "Hold on. I'm not done making out with my girlfriend." Then he pulled me against him and kissed me, being thoroughly obvious with his tongue and the groping of my butt. When he finally pulled away, Cameron was still standing there, staring.

"That supposed to impress me?" he asked, and went into the classroom.

My face was hot, and not because the kiss was so great. "Why did you do that, Ethan?"

"Because I wanted to." His face was as red as mine felt.

"In the future, I'd appreciate it if you didn't use my body to make a point." The final bell rang; I pushed past him and went straight to my seat, pulled out my government book, and bit the inside of my cheek so I wouldn't cry. I hadn't cried at school since the day I heard Cameron died. Not crying at school was a key aspect of being Jenna Vaughn.

Mr. O'Connor made the mistake of being nice, coming up to me during a pop quiz to whisper, "Everything okay, Jenna?"

I shook my head.

"Would you like a hall pass?"

I nodded.

He went back to his desk, wrote me a pass, and brought it to me with everyone watching. Everyone except Ethan, who refused to look at me.

Leaning against the bathroom stall I had a total Jennifer Harris moment. I'd lost count of the number of times I'd cried at school back then for any and every reason: dropping my juice box on the playground, Mrs. Jameson accidentally sitting on my papier-mâché project, losing the rubber ball that went with my set of jacks.

Baby. Big fat baby.

"Sensitive," "emotional," "dramatic" were the words adults used.

They seemed to think it was something I should be able to get a grip on. "You're going to have to learn to pull yourself together, Jennifer" was what Principal Anderson said once after one of my episodes.

I ran a paper towel under the faucet and pressed it to my face, looking in the mirror to check the status of the redness of my eyes. *Baby.* Then a voice from underneath that, one I hadn't heard before, talked back. *You're not a baby. Babies don't tear away window screens with their bare hands to save themselves.* I closed my eyes, wanting to hear more, trying to block out any image of Jenna Vaughn that obscured my view of Jennifer Harris. But apparently she'd finished talking.

Cameron wasn't in detention, though he'd been late, too. I wasn't surprised; he seemed to operate by his own rules, even with the school administration. Ethan was waiting for me outside the room when it was over; I pretended not to see him and went the other way. "Where are you going?" he asked, turning around when he realized I wasn't tagging along.

"I have to get home early. My mom needs me to do some stuff around the house."

"What about the play?"

I looked at him. I knew he was embarrassed and sorry for the scene outside government. And I knew that he expected me, as usual, to silently forgive him and act like everything was A-OK, restoring the balance of our little universe with a smile or a hug. But I couldn't. "I'll have to miss it today," I said. "Sorry."

He shrugged, obviously angry. "Whatever. We're just making the final casting decisions. No big deal."

"Well. Have fun."

"Jenna . . ."

"What, Ethan?" I said it fast, annoyed.

"Never mind. God. What's *wrong* with you lately?" He started to walk away, then looked back. "Oh, let me guess. Hormones, right? Why don't you go home and take some Midol."

"Yeah. I'll do that."

Cameron stood by my car in the student lot. "How come you weren't in detention?" I asked, digging in my backpack for my keys.

He shrugged. "I'll make it up tomorrow."

My hands closed around my key chain, the one with the Statue of Liberty that Ethan had brought back from a family trip to New York right before school started. I wondered how much longer I'd keep it. "Do you need a ride?"

"No."

I sighed. "Then what are you doing here?" He stared at the ground and I finally instructed him to get in the car. He obeyed, folding himself into the seat. We pulled out of the lot and I drove for a few blocks before asking him where we were going, even though I already knew what he wanted — to go back to where it had all begun. "I don't think I'm ready, Cameron."

"Come on," he said. "It will be okay."

We were at a stoplight; I glanced at him, wanting him to just say okay, we didn't have to go, to suggest something else like a drive up one of the canyons, or sharing a plate of cheese fries. I wished, in that moment, that we could simply have a normal friendship based on the usual things instead of on our shared and individual histories of feeling like we didn't belong in our lives.

The light turned green and Cameron asked, "Trust me, Jennifer. Just . . . trust me."

I drove another block or two. "Why should I?"

"Why shouldn't you?"

Because you left me, Cameron. After everything we went through. But I knew it wasn't his fault, any more than it was mine. It wasn't like either of us had control over our lives. We were at the mercy of our parents, both of us. Anyway, I'd already turned the car toward the freeway entrance. I turned on the car radio and we drove twenty minutes without talking. When the exit finally came into view, ugly warehouses and the new Wal-Mart looming before us, I said, "Let's go to my old apartment first. I haven't been there since we moved."

"I've gone by it a couple of times."

"Really?"

"Yeah. Living there with you was kind of my best memory."

I imagined that, him going to the apartment and looking up at the window and thinking about me.

We were getting close. The area looked nicer in some ways, if you liked shiny chain stores and restaurants and mall developments. When I finally recognized my old street, my heart sped up. "There it is," I said. Nearly everything at the old apartment building was the same — same beige paint, same carports with their rusting tin roofs, same cement walkways surrounded by too-green grass and man-made ponds. Now there were also yellow and green flags along the street like exclamation points, announcing the alleged fabulousness of life at West Valley Cove & Gardens.

"Move-in special," Cameron said, pointing to a banner over the entry gate. "First month's rent free."

"So tempting." We parked, and walked on the cement path toward building C, on the side of the property our window had faced. We'd had a lovely view of storage units, which I would stare out at every day after school. Now, my breath caught when I rounded the corner. They'd planted a small grove of aspens where there had been a dry, empty stretch of ground between me and the storage units. Like magic, the aspens were full grown, their leaves just turning from the green of late summer to the gold of fall. What would it have been like, I wondered, to look out at those white-barked trees every day instead of a dead lot of nothing?

A gentle wind came up and the leaves quaked. "Listen," I said to Cameron.

He hopped over the fake stream running between us and the stand of trees. I did the same, and we walked deeper in. "They clatter," he said. "The leaves clatter. Remember?"

I sat on the ground and then lay back. "Come on. Like we used to."

The wind got stronger, and he stretched out next to me, arm's length apart. We stayed like that, listening, for a long time.

"What are you thinking?" he asked.

I closed my eyes. "So many things."

"Like?"

"My mom told me about what really happened when I thought you died. I want to know what it was like to live in a shelter, and why you were sleeping in my car this morning. I want to know where you live now and what your life has been like for the last eight years and why you came back. Why you really came back. I want to know what was going on in your house and if what your dad did that day was . . ." I swallowed. "If it was the kind of thing he did a lot. To you." I exhaled and opened my eyes. "That's what I'm thinking."

Before he could answer, my cell phone beeped the opening notes of Beethoven's Fifth Symphony. I pulled it from my jacket pocket and saw Ethan's number on the screen. I turned off the phone. My back was getting cold and damp but I didn't move, just in case Cameron was about to answer even one of my questions. But he stood and stared down at me, extending a hand to help me up. "Let's go check out the school."

"That's all you have to say?"

He was lit from behind by the afternoon sun, green-gold under the aspens. Maybe it was the sun or the fact that I had barely eaten that day, but the aspens seemed to spin around him in slow motion and I wanted to stay there forever and never go back to Jones Hall, never go back to Ethan. There was something inviting and consoling about the scenario Mom had posed: Cameron as my only friend, for all those years, my whole life. Just us enduring everything together with complete understanding and unquestioning loyalty, in a world that only we occupied. I wouldn't have to fake anything anymore. I could see now, staring up at him, that it wouldn't be so hard to slip back into that life, leaving everything I'd built as Jenna Vaughn behind.

He crouched down next to me. I put my hand on the hem of his jeans. It was the first time I'd touched him since that day in the cafeteria line.

"I've got so much to tell you," he said, so quietly I almost couldn't hear. "Been thinking about how to even start."

"Start anywhere," I whispered. "I just want to know."

"I feel like I've already told you everything, in a way. I've been talking to you in my head for eight years, writing epics and sequels to epics, and sequels to the sequels."

I let my fingers move down to the laces of his boots, then up to the top of his sock. One more millimeter and my fingertip would be against his skin. I moved it back down, resting on the knob of his ankle. "I'm here now," I said. "You can talk to me, right out loud."

Just then, two boys, eight or nine years old, crashed into the grove, leaping over the stream like we had. They froze when they saw us; I jerked my hand away from Cameron's ankle and sat up.

"Oh," one boy said, "hi."

"Hi," I said. "We were just leaving." I got up without Cameron's help, brushed myself off, and followed him back to the parking lot.

At our old elementary school, it was Cameron who led the way across the blacktop, past basketball hoops and swings where a few kids still played. I knew where he was headed — straight to the bench outside Mr. Lloyd's room.

"I remember sitting here," he said, "and watching you over there." He pointed, but I didn't have to look. Before Cameron and I got close, I spent a lot of lunches the same way, starting off eating and reading on my special bench on the other side of the yard, followed by walking the perimeter of the playground, balancing on the small cement curb that separated the blacktop from the landscaping, around and around and around, hoping I looked busy and like it didn't matter that I had no friends.

I sat next to Cameron on the bench. "What did you think when you used to watch me?"

He leaned his head against the building. "That I understood you. That you'd understand me."

"Do you remember the first time you talked to me? Because I don't. I've been trying to remember for years and I can't get it."

"You don't remember? Wasn't me that talked to you. You talked to me."

I scooted forward on the bench and looked at him. "I did?"

"You walked right across the yard here at recess," he said, pointing. "Came straight up to me." He laughed. "You looked so determined. I was scared you were gonna kick me in the shins or something."

I didn't remember this at all, any of it.

"You said you were starting a club," he continued. "Asked me if I wanted to join."

"Wait . . ." Something was there, at the very edge of my memory, coming into focus. "Do you remember if it happened to be May Day?"

"That the one with the pole and all the ribbons?"

"Yes!"

"Yep. All the girls had ribbons in their hair but you."

Jordana wouldn't let me wear ribbons. She said my hair was too greasy and I might give someone lice, and somehow I submitted to her logic. "I do remember," I said softly. "I haven't thought of that in forever. I kept thinking you were the one to make friends with me first."

"Nope." He smiled. "You started this whole thing. I wanted to, but you were the one with the guts to actually do it."

"I think of myself as being a coward, and a baby, scared all the time."

He got quiet. We watched kids in the schoolyard playing basketball. "You're not," he finally said. "You know that." He got up suddenly. "Let's go. We got one more stop."

It took awhile for us to find it, the streets looking the same block after block, just endless rows of boring homes in various shades of beige, taupe, gray, and ivory. The air in the car changed, got tense. Conversation stopped and it wasn't the comfortable silence anymore but the kind of silence that makes you want to say something, anything. The closer we got to his house, the more it got like that. I could see Cameron, from the corner of my eye, gripping the inside passenger door handle, his fingers going white.

I didn't feel so great myself.

"Here," he said, his voice flat and detached.

We were in front of a run-down ranch-style house with tan siding and a big, dead lawn. I left the engine running. My heart pounded. "We don't have to do this," I said.

His jaw set in a way that reminded me of how he'd look sometimes back in grade school, standing around the fringes of a kickball game or on that bench by Mr. Lloyd's room. "We do, though."

I shook my head, staring at the house. Right then, a woman walked out, carrying a bag of trash. "Let's ask her if we can go in," Cameron said.

"Go *in?*"

He turned to me. "Yeah."

I lowered my voice to a whisper. "Shouldn't we, like, talk about it first? About what happened?"

"Why? We know what happened."

"I can't."

"But I'm with you. We're together."

My eyes filled. He looked out the window. The woman went back in the house and closed the door. "We can come back some other time," I said, "after we've talked." I put the car in drive. "Let's go somewhere. Coffee. Something."

"Doesn't matter." His jaw was set again, his voice dead flat.

"It *does* matter, Cameron. That's the point. If it didn't matter I could just go in right now. I'm not ready. You can't just show up af-

126

ter all these years and expect me to be *ready*." He opened the door and started to get out. "Wait, where are you going?"

"Sorry I came here and messed up your life."

"That's not what I said!" But he was out of the car, walking down the block, away from me.

CHAPTER 16

WHEN I GOT HOME, I WENT STRAIGHT TO MY ROOM. IT TOOK
more than an hour to recover from the nausea and the on-again,
off-again crying that started every time I thought about Cameron's
face, the tone of his voice, the sight of him getting out of the car.
I was hurt, then angry. Then guilty for feeling angry. Then angry
for feeling guilty. And so on. I lay on my bed with a cold wash-
cloth over my eyes to remove all evidence of tears. I took mental
inventory of the refrigerator and cupboards in case there was anything there that could make me feel better. But that's not really
what I wanted. What I wanted was to feel like Jenna Vaughn again.
So when I was reasonably in control of myself, I picked up my cell
and dialed Ethan.

"Hi," I said. "Sorry I missed your call before."

"How come you didn't call me back?"

"You didn't leave a message."

"But you knew I called."

"I'm calling you back now." I could hear his breath, him starting to say something and then changing his mind. "I'm sorry," I said quickly, "for that and for being cranky today."

"Well. I just wanted to tell you that we have a cast list." He sounded relieved and like himself. "Steph gets the part she wants. No surprise there. You know Jill Stevenson? That sophomore? She got the other lead."

"What about Katy?"

"Katy's in it, since she'd never forgive me if I left her out, but she didn't exactly show a lot of ambition."

"You know she'll do a good job in the end," I said, trying to keep up a believable impression of me, to sound like I cared about the school play. "So. Rehearsals start tomorrow?"

"Just a table reading," he said. "You should come. Cast bonding and whatnot."

"Okay."

"Sorry. About earlier today."

I curled into a ball on my bed and sighed. "It's okay."

"Really?"

Well, no, not really. But at least Ethan wouldn't jump out of my car without explanation. "Yeah," I said.

"Can I come over?"

I considered. "Not tonight. Tomorrow? My parents are going to a wine tasting."

"Tomorrow. 'Night, Jenna."

"'Night."

• • •

At dinner, Mom asked me about Cameron, where he was living and where his brothers and sisters were going to school and if I had their number. She wanted to call his mom, have them all over for dinner. I realized I had the answers to none of her questions.

"I have a number for Cameron's cell," I said. "That's all."

"Would you call him tonight? Find out how to get in touch with his mom? We'll make a day of it," she said, getting excited. "One last barbecue before the first snow."

Alan watched me. "If that's okay with you," he said.

Mom waved her fork dismissively. "Of course it's okay with her!" She turned to me. "I've been thinking, since our talk. When I first saw that Cameron was back, I admit I had concerns about what that would do to you. Now I think it will be good for us to have them back in our lives, the whole family."

"Wait wait wait," Alan started. "Honey, I —"

"What?"

"Mom, I don't even remember his mother or his brothers and sisters. I never knew them."

"Maybe you should. Maybe it would help you understand Cameron and the whole situation."

"I understand him," I said. "And the 'whole situation.'"

"I don't think you do."

"Well, you don't know everything."

"I think I know more than you do," she said. "Remember, I heard it all from his mother and —"

"Okay," I said. "Fine. You know more than I do. I'll call him. I'll tell him to invite everyone over for a family reunion." I stood up and cleared my plate. "I'd love to talk about this more, but I have a ton of homework."

She called after me, "I didn't mean to upset you . . ."

As I closed the door to my room, I heard Alan: "Give her time to think."

A noise woke me again. This time it was definitely not a raccoon or a cat, unless a raccoon or cat had learned how to tap on my window. I knew before opening the curtains who it was. I inched the window up. This time, we were unhindered by a screen.

"Cameron," I whispered, "what are you doing?"

He folded his arms on the sill. "I want to talk."

"Now?"

"You don't have to let me in if you don't want, but there's a lot I should tell you. Ask me anything you want and I'll answer."

"But . . . now? You couldn't just call?"

"Didn't think you'd answer my call after what I did today."

I shivered from the cold air pouring in through the window. "Okay." He hoisted himself up to crawl through, and there he was, right in my room. I got back in bed, sitting up with the covers tucked around me, and turned on the bedside lamp.

He closed the window. "This isn't the kind of room I pictured you in," he said, looking around at my big bed, and the overstuffed chair and ottoman in the corner where I did all my reading, my desk and computer, the wine-colored paint on the walls contrasting with the white of the ceiling.

"Cameron . . ."

"It's nice." He sat in the armchair. The cuffs of his jeans were damp and his boots dirty.

"Take off your boots," I said. "Please." He did, and his socks, and then put his bare feet up on the ottoman. The soles were rough but clean. I started: "My mom was asking me tonight about your mom, and your brothers and sisters. She wants them all to come over. Like to celebrate your miraculous return."

"My mom's in California. Whole family's there, except me."

Somehow this did not shock me. Cameron didn't act like a regular teenager who lived at home with parents and rules and people taking care of him. "Where do you live? I mean, last night you're sleeping in my car, tonight you're lurking around my house at two in the morning. Are you . . . homeless or something?"

He laughed. "I take care of myself. Have since I was fifteen. I work. I pay rent. You heard of emancipated minors? That's me."

"Like when you divorce your parents? I thought only child actors did that."

"Nope." He leaned his head against the back of the chair. "Mind if we turn out the light? Seems bright."

I did. "There's a blanket on the back of the chair if you need it."

"Thanks." His outline moved in the dark, and I heard the sounds of him settling in.

"But your mom *left* your dad," I said. "My mom said you all went to a shelter and hid from him and everything. I thought you started a new life. Why did you move out?"

"She went back to him. And then left him again. And then went back. And left. On and on. They've been divorced a long time, but she still lets him come around the house and stay over and tell the kids what to do and all that. They had two more kids together after the divorce. Still thinks he's the man of the house." He paused there, his voice getting quieter. "Like he knows what a man really is. Makes me sick."

"Why did you come back to Salt Lake?" I knew the answer before I asked the question and he knew I knew, and it was like you could see the shadow of it hanging there between us.

"I needed to see you," he finally said. "It's hard to explain."

"You don't have to."

"I tried telling my mom once what happened that day. Showed her the hole in the window screen and Moe and even after that she said it was complicated, that my dad's a complicated man and we all needed to try harder to understand him." His voice was shaking now. "And I thought, hey, maybe she's right. Maybe he was just playing around, you know. Maybe we didn't need to run."

"We did," I whispered.

"That's why I had to come, see?" He didn't move and I didn't move, but in a few seconds I heard him sniffling and he couldn't stop and I knew he was crying. "Cameron." I propped myself up, reached out my arm. "Come here." He got up and came to me, dragging his blanket behind him like a child. I scooted over in my bed to make room. "Come on."

He positioned himself beside me — I stayed under the covers, he was on top of them, his head next to mine on the pillow. I stroked his hair and thought of the week he'd lived at our house, the way we slept shoulder to shoulder in our sleeping bags in the living room, and I got another good memory.

Jennifer, Cameron had said. *You awake?*

His voice was coming from across the room. I sat up. *Yeah.*

Look. He was standing by the living room window. The blinds were closed, but he had his hands on the cord, a big smile on his face. *Ready?*

I nodded, starting to smile myself.

One, two, three, Cameron said, then pulled the blind up, hand over hand on the cord like someone on TV. His smile got even bigger as he watched my face.

Snow. Giant flakes of it falling in front of the window even though it was only September.

Now, I fell asleep with my arm over Cameron's chest, thinking of how the flakes had been slow and white in the glow of the streetlights that lined the apartment walkways, and the smile on his face and on mine, like the snow was personal, a gift he'd given me himself.

Alan, as per his usual routine, got up early and peeked into my room to check on me. What he found were his teenage stepdaughter and her childhood sweetheart curled up in the same bed, sound asleep and draped all over each other. He hissed my name, alarmed: "Jenna!"

"Wha —?" I sat straight up, immediately aware of what was happening and how it all looked. I clambered over Cameron, who was just coming to consciousness, and followed Alan into the kitchen.

"It's nothing, I swear," I said in a whisper. If Mom wasn't up yet, I wanted to keep it that way.

Alan shook his head. "It looks bad." He glanced toward my bedroom. "Was that Ethan? Tell him to come out here. I want to talk to him."

"Um, it's not Ethan. It's Cameron."

He put his hands to his head. "Jenna. Jenna."

"I know. Is Mom awake?"

"Not yet."

I kept my voice low. "Can we talk by the fish tank?"

He led, I followed.

"He came to my window in the night," I explained. "He needed to talk. I let him in. It was me. It was my idea. It was all . . . nothing happened."

"This isn't my *area*," Alan said, looking at the fish. "Your mom is supposed to do the tough stuff. We have a policy of laissez-faire when it comes to me and . . . this kind of thing."

"Exactly. So," I said hopefully, "go make the coffee and we'll pretend nothing ever happened."

Cameron came into the room, his blanket wrapped around him. His hair was sticking up in the back, and his long eyelashes hooded sleepy eyes. "I just needed to talk to someone," he said to Alan. "Guess we fell asleep."

"Uh-huh." Alan cast an anxious glance toward his and my mom's bedroom and said, "You couldn't talk in the kitchen?"

"We didn't think about it," I said. "That's how innocent it was, see?"

Alan stared at us, still shaking his head. "Look, Cameron, just get out of here before Jenna's mom sees you. Okay?"

He nodded. "I'll go get my boots."

I breathed a sigh of relief. "*Thank* you, Alan."

When Cameron shut my bedroom door, Alan said, "Jenna. This is the kind of situation that's very, very *awkward*, to say the least. If your mom were to find out, I would be in scalding hot water."

"She won't. Thank you thank you thank you."

"Now. I need my coffee." He shuffled off to the kitchen, ankles cracking. "I'm too old for this."

Back in my room, I watched Cameron get ready to go, thinking about everything we'd talked about and what it meant. "Where do you live?" I asked. "I'll take you home."

"I share a studio apartment with three other guys. It's a dump," he said, lacing up his boots.

"How come you were sleeping in my car yesterday?"

"Sometimes I don't want to be there." He pulled on his jacket. "I'll go straight to school, shower in the locker room. See you later." He started to open the window.

"Wait," I said. "You can use the front door, you know. Just be quiet."

"Okay." He paused on his way out of my room, looking back once to say, "Thanks."

CHAPTER 17

CAMERON AND I PRETENDED NOT TO NOTICE EACH OTHER during homeroom. I did stare at the back of his head and think about how it had been on my pillow only a couple hours earlier, and wondered if Alan would really not tell, and if it was the kind of thing that was likely to ever happen again.

Katy walked with me to first period, peppering me with questions about Cameron.

"Steph said he's going to work on the play," she said excitedly. "Which is perfect because I can get to know him, but you have to give me some insider info. What's he like? Has he dated a lot of girls? I mean, is he a player, or what?"

"No," I said, "he's not a player."

"Did you guys ever kiss? What's his type? Does he like redheads?"

"I don't know." I noticed she looked nice considering it was a regular school day — her hair twisted up, makeup done, looking smart and dramatic in a black turtleneck and wire-rim glasses instead of her contacts. She'd dressed up for a boy who had spent the night sleeping next to me. "He's only been here a week, and before that I hadn't seen him in eight years. He's probably totally different."

She sighed, impatient. "Okay, then, what *was* he like? Just give me something to go on so that I have a shot at him!"

"A 'shot at him'? Are you on an elk hunt?"

"What's the problem, Jenna?" She'd come to a complete stop in the hall; people walked around us. "Is it so awful for me to want to have a boyfriend? It is so impossible to believe it could happen?"

"Katy, don't. I didn't mean it like that. Come on." I took her arm, tried to pull her along toward class. She jerked it away.

"You've obviously forgotten what it feels like to be single. If this had happened last year, you'd be helping me." Suddenly she was crying. I led her to the side of the hallway.

"I'm sorry, Katy. Really."

"You never call me anymore," she said, wiping her eyes. "I'm used to Steph dumping me for boys, but not you."

I had no defense. I'd barely noticed Katy since starting to date Ethan. "We'll get to spend a lot of time together during the play, at least. . . ." The final bell rang; I was in for my second detention of the week.

"Jenna, you have to help me get Cameron," she said. "You *have* to. He'll listen to you."

"I don't know if he's interested in having a girlfriend right now." She sniffed back her last tears and ran her finger under her eyes to clean up mascara smudges. "But I'll do my best," I said. "Okay?"

"That's all I'm asking."

• • •

Ethan and I went off campus for lunch, eating in his car at Liberty Park and then spending the last ten minutes making out. Usually making out was a good distraction, but I couldn't turn the thinking part of my brain off. What did it mean that I'd spent the night next to Cameron? Anything?

After a while, Ethan brought my mind back into focus when he murmured into my neck, "You're so . . . mm."

"So are you."

"I'm coming over tonight, right? Your parents will be gone?"

I sat up and straightened my shirt. "Yeah. But I have a ton of homework. So we have to concentrate. On the homework, I mean."

He laughed. "You're funny."

I made a scoffing noise.

"What?"

I turned to him and rested my head on the back of the seat. "When I was a kid," I said, "I always thought of funny stuff in my head but I never said it."

"Why not?"

"Because no one was listening."

He moved his hand to my neck, rubbing it gently. "I would have listened."

"I don't think so."

"Would, too," he said, teasing.

"I wasn't the kind of person you would have liked." My eyes

stung. "Think of the most unpopular kid you've ever known. The one who got picked on and ignored, every day."

"Come on, I bet you weren't like that."

No one, of course, wants to believe that his girlfriend — the girl he just made out with — was the gross, fat kid who sat alone in the corner of the school yard. But I kept talking. Maybe it was guilt over Cameron sleeping in my bed, or what Steph had said about me resisting a Katy/Cameron matchup because I wanted him for myself. Or maybe I was trying to push Ethan away, or toward me, or somewhere. Anything to alter the current inertia of our relationship. "I was," I said. "I was exactly like that. You wouldn't have listened to me. You wouldn't have even looked at me."

"Well." He took his hand off of my neck and looked out the car window, proving my point. Even the thought of me back then with the present me right in front of him was enough to make him avert his eyes. "That's the past. You should just . . . forget that stuff. It never happened." Having wiped his mind clear of my previous existence, he turned back to me. "You're here now, and you're you."

"Am I me?"

"What do you mean? Of course you're you. Who else would you be?"

Good question. "We better go. I don't need another detention."

He gave me a kiss. "Sometimes you think too much."

I think that was the beginning of the end.

• • •

I made it all the way to my car after school before remembering about rehearsal. I hurried back to the drama room, where Ethan, Mr. Bingry, and the cast were sitting in a circle with their scripts. Ethan glanced up when I walked in, smiled, then looked back at his script.

My purpose in being there was not exactly clear. There were no extra seats at the table, so whatever Ethan had meant by me being part of "cast bonding" was not readily apparent. I lurked nearby for a minute waiting for some kind of instructions, but none came so I sat in the nearest chair and took out a notebook and pen in case I was actually called upon to do something. Finally, halfway through, Mr. Bingry called for a break. Ethan ran off to the bathroom and Bingry waggled his finger at me. I went over to him. "Start making a prop list," he said. "This play has a lot of them."

"It would help if I had a script. So that I knew what said props actually were."

"Ethan didn't give you a script?" Bingry sighed and shuffled through a stack in front of him. "Here."

I took it and flipped through, trying not to be irritated that Ethan had failed to help me do my job. "What's my budget?"

"Beg, borrow, or steal everything that you can."

I wrote "zero budget" in my notebook. "I can probably get stuff from my house. My mom will never notice."

"That's the spirit."

Ethan came back in, giving me a wave before sitting down at the cast table again. They were all laughing about something. Bonding. I retreated to my offstage chair and thought about lunch in the park, and how Ethan had not only told me to forget my past but shown me that he didn't want to hear about it, didn't even want to know about it.

I sat in the school parking lot longer than I needed to, just in case Cameron came looking for me or for a ride or for a talk or for anything. I'd tried his cell phone but it went straight to voice mail. I was ready to go back to his old house. I was ready to do anything at all to stay close to him.

CHAPTER 18

WHEN I GOT HOME FROM SCHOOL THERE WAS HALF A COFFEE cake on the kitchen table. Mom and Alan must have been eating it that morning and I hadn't noticed because I was too busy freaking out over Alan discovering Cameron in my bed. I hadn't binged since Sunday night in the Crown Burgers parking lot. But I stared at the coffee cake and imagined how it would taste with a glass of milk. And then I saw my mom's favorite coffee cup on the table, with a little milky coffee left in it, and imagined how it would be to sit down with her and share a piece of cake and talk, actually talk about things that mattered.

The longing for her in that moment was an ache in my chest and fingertips, as strong as anything I'd ever felt. I wanted to talk to tell her about what had happened at Cameron's house that day, and everything else about what it was like to be me when she was so busy and I was so hidden. I wanted to tell her how it felt to walk around the school yard in circles while I watched Jordana and her friends play, and then what it meant — what it really, really meant — to get that ring in my lunch box from Cameron, how he'd saved me, and then how I'd saved us.

Here I was all over again, alone in an empty house after school. I could have paged my mom and she'd call me right back but then what would I say? *Hi. I have to tell you about something that happened to me when I was nine. And by the way, I miss you, have missed you my whole life.* That was not a conversation you could have on the phone at work. Anyway, I'd learned how to get along without her when I didn't have any other options; it was a habit easier kept than broken.

So I ate the coffee cake instead, and cleaned up all the evidence, and fell asleep in front of the TV. When I woke up, Mom and Alan were standing over me, dressed up with purse and car keys, respectively, in hand. "Honey? Jenna. We're leaving now, okay?"

I lifted my stiff neck. "What time is it?"

"About quarter to seven," Mom said. "You were just snoring away so we let you sleep."

My mouth was filmy, one hand tingling from being slept on. Alan gazed down and asked, "Everything okay? We can always stay home if you want."

I shook my head. "I'm fine." I needed them out of there so I could get ready for Ethan. I sat up and stretched. "You'd better go so you can get a parking spot."

They left. I checked my cell to see if Cameron had called. He hadn't.

In the bathroom, I brushed and brushed my teeth, washed my face and hands, changed. I needed a whole shower but there wasn't time. The doorbell rang and Ethan was there.

"Hey," I said, giving him a quick kiss, trying to feel happy to see him.

"I hope you got your homework done." He went straight for me, kissing my neck and squeezing my waist. I pushed him off me.

"No, I didn't. I haven't even started it." I turned and walked to the kitchen table where my books were stacked. I sat down and opened my trig. He followed.

"Well I already did mine," he said, tossing his floppy bangs, which were starting to annoy me. "I'm finished. Done."

I flipped through my book, the pages making sharp cracks with every turn. "I *told* you that I had a ton. I told you that."

"I thought you were, like, kidding around."

I stared at him. "Why did you think that? Look," I said waving my hands over my books, "I have a crapload of stuff to get done and I'm practically flunking trig. I really need to get to work."

He sulked, and roamed around the kitchen randomly opening cupboards. "Do you have any food around here? Let's order a pizza."

"No."

"I'll pay for it."

"No!" I slammed my pencil down on the table. "Ethan, can you pay attention to someone other than yourself for one minute?"

He spun around. "What? I'm *hungry*. Sue me."

He was still cute, still infinitely kissable. But I didn't feel anything. What did our three months add up to, anyway? A bunch of making out and occasionally going somewhere and IM-ing late at night. Even by thinking in terms of three months I knew Ethan and I, our couplehood, was a finite thing. The measuring of time meant there would be an end. If we broke up, would I still be able to sit at our lunch table every day? Katy would be mad. Steph would think I was stupid. Gil and the Daves probably wouldn't think of me at all.

"It's just that I told you I had a lot of homework," I said. "And you know trig is hard for me. And you didn't give me an *Odd Couple* script when you were supposed to and I don't even know why I had to be at the rehearsal today when you barely acknowledged my presence."

"Because you're the stage manager."

"Which I didn't ask to be. You volunteered me."

"Because I wanted you to be there with me! I knew you wouldn't audition, so at least this way we could still be hanging out." He came over to me and started rubbing my shoulders. I tolerated it until he said, "Don't get mad. Let's, like, put on some music and lie between the speakers and cuddle and stuff."

I wrenched my neck away. "Oh my *God,* Ethan! Have you not heard one word I said?"

"What is *up* with you, Jenna? You've been a moody bitch ever since your birthday. Ever since Cameron showed up." He went into the living room. I followed. "I'm gonna go," he said, pulling his coat on. He stopped at the door and turned back, as if waiting for me to say something. I couldn't speak, just shook my head and kept my arms folded across me, and he walked out.

I went straight to my room, turned on the light, and let out a yelp.

Cameron was sitting in my armchair. I backed a little way into the hall.

"It's okay," he said, "it's just me."

"It's *not* okay," I said, my voice trembling both from the fight with Ethan and the shock of seeing Cameron. "It is so not okay."

"Sorry. I was gonna ring the bell, but I saw Ethan coming and ducked down the side of the house."

"And then crawled in my *window?*" He was silent. I wondered if he'd heard Ethan and me in the kitchen, was sure he had, since I could usually hear everything in the kitchen from my room and we weren't exactly keeping the volume down. "What do you want, Cameron?"

"Don't be mad."

"I'm not."

"You are."

"Okay, I am." I sighed. "But I'm also happy to see you." And I was. I sat on my bed, thinking how nice it would be to have Cameron lying next to me again. I'd hardly had time to enjoy it, experience it, the first time. "I just think you should use the door."

"I need to borrow your car."

"Um, okay," I said slowly. "I'm not supposed to let anyone else drive it. It's an insurance thing and a house rule."

"What if it's an emergency?"

"Where do you need to go?" I asked. "I can take you." Clearly I was not destined to do homework.

"My apartment, to get some stuff."

"Fine. Let's go." I got up; he didn't move.

"You can't. It's dangerous. My roommates are dangerous."

"What do you mean, dangerous?"

"I haven't paid rent. In a while. They're gonna be pissed." He looked down. "Don't want you to have to deal with the crap in my life. Not again."

"What's it going to take to convince you that you haven't ruined my life?" I said, frustrated. "Not then, not now."

He rubbed his nose with the back of his wrist, just like a little kid. "I don't know."

I sat back down. "How long have you been here, anyway, that you haven't paid rent 'in a while'?"

"Since August. I thought I'd get a job, find you, get my own place. Then I couldn't find work at first and thought it wouldn't kill me to finish school. I've been working here and there, but didn't know how fast my money would run out." He finally stood. "Point is, they have my stuff. My pictures. My letters. My life. All I have."

August. He'd been right in Salt Lake at least two months before contacting me. He'd been there before things got really serious with Ethan. What if he'd made himself known sooner? "I'll take you," I said. "Then what happens after you get your stuff? I can't just leave you on the streets."

"I can sleep in your car again, maybe? And then come in early for a shower before your parents are even up?"

He might have been tall and strong. He might have been independent — an emancipated minor, a working man who paid his way. But all I could see when I looked at Cameron Quick was someone who needed taking care of. And there was no one to do it but me.

"Let's go," I said. "When we get back we'll wait up for my parents. And talk to them about . . . all this."

It was dark out, and a little drizzly. We drove down the hills of the Avenues and into downtown. Cameron gave directions; I turned and turned and turned again.

"Pull over here," he said when we'd reached the edges of the Rose Park neighborhood, notorious for gangs and a sludge pit that the federal government had to come clean up. "It's down the street a little bit," he said, pointing to a falling-apart fourplex with a pile of tires in the front yard. "Wait in the car." He opened the door and started to climb out.

"Hold on! How long should I give you? What if you don't come back in a certain number of minutes? Should I call the cops?"

"Don't do anything. Don't call anyone. I'll be fine."

"But what if you're not?"

"Then go home."

And with that, he got out and jogged down the street, like if I heard screams or gunshots or whatever I would just drive on home like nothing happened. Well, good for you, I thought, watching him climb a short cement staircase and put a key in the door. You don't need anyone. Fine.

I watched the clock. Three minutes went by, four. I thought about knocking on the door, having of course no idea what I would actually do once I got there. Maybe I'd have to break the door down, wrestle Cameron away from the bad men, and then carry him out the way you hear people when they get a huge burst of adrenaline. Except the person I pictured rescuing was little Cameron, in shorts and a striped T-shirt, his arms wrapped around my neck.

Then there he was, bursting out of the apartment door and bounding down the steps, a big garbage bag in hand. He ran to the car, fast. I reached over and opened the passenger door and he jumped in.

"*Go.*"

You can't exactly peel out in a '94 Escort, but I did my best. Cameron breathed hard, clutching the garbage bag to his chest.

"What *happened?*" I drove a good fifteen miles per hour over the speed limit, convinced we were being chased by angry roommates with guns.

"Nothing. You can slow down."

I didn't. "Nothing? Nothing happened?"

"They weren't even there."

Then I did slow down. "No one was there? At all?"

"Right." His breathing had returned to almost normal.

"Then what's the deal with freaking me out like that?" My voice came out high and hysterical and I realized how nervous I'd been, imagining some dangerous scenario from which Cameron had barely escaped, an echo of that day at his house.

"I don't know. I started to picture one of them pulling up and finding me there and . . . I panicked." He rummaged through the garbage bag in his lap angrily. "My tools were gone. They probably already sold them."

"Tools?"

"How I make my living. Or *made* my living in California. Handyman stuff, day labor for subcontractors. Like that."

I thought about the dollhouse. I wanted to say something like, *Yeah, you've always been good at that, like with the dollhouse.* But we still hadn't discussed any details of that day, so I didn't say anything. Cameron interpreted my silence as something else.

"I know it's not like being a nurse or a college professor like your parents, but it's what I can do and people always need stuff fixed and built. Even if it's all I do the rest of my life there's no shame in it. You can make good money doing that, you know."

"I think it's great," I said. "You're smart enough for college, though. Look how fast you're catching up at Jones. You could do anything you want."

"What about you? What are you going to do?"

I shrugged. "I'll just go to the U. I can get a tuition discount through Alan. I'll probably be an English teacher or something." Not that I'd given it much thought lately. I'd just sort of always assumed that's what I'd do, English being the only subject I remotely cared about or was any good at.

"At least you know what you want. I don't know what I want." Then he was quiet for a long time. We were almost home before he said, "Just want to be with you. Like this."

My heart sped up. I made a joke. "That's probably not a viable career option."

"Yeah," he said, laughing a little. "Probably not."

By the time Mom and Alan got home, Cameron was asleep on the couch and I was attempting to get at least a little homework done before bed. Concentrating was impossible, so I typed an English paper that was already pretty much done.

I heard them come in the back door and met them in the kitchen. They looked rosy and happy from wine and snacks. I jumped right in: "So, Cameron is asleep on the couch. And basically he's homeless."

Mom blinked a few times. "Excuse me?"

"He's emancipated from his parents." I was matter-of-fact, just like she had been when she'd told me the Quick family saga. Also, the complicated drama of everything that had gone on that evening had worn me down; I'd switched myself nearly off. "Right now he can't pay his rent. Because he's trying to finish school."

"What about his mother?" Mom asked. "What about his brothers and sisters, his family?"

"They're in California. His dad is still with them, too."

"You're kidding."

"Hm," Alan said. It was a loaded "hm," no doubt because the image of Cameron sleeping in my room was fresh in his mind. "I'm not too sure about this."

"Well, we have to let him stay here tonight," Mom said, glancing toward the living room, "clearly. It's late and we're all tired and we can deal with this tomorrow."

Alan looked at her, unconvinced. "He's a big, grown guy, honey, whom we know little about. And we have a teenage daughter."

"Well, I *do* know him," Mom insisted, "and there's nothing to worry about."

Alan opened his mouth like he might be about to tell her about the bedroom incident. I interrupted, "Really, Alan, there's not."

He continued, starting to sound a little annoyed, "What I was *going* to ask is how do we know he's emancipated? How do we know he's not just a runaway? What is our responsibility here if we let him stay?"

"Trust me," Mom said, unwinding her scarf like the issue was all settled. "If there's one teenager in the world with legitimate reason to divorce his parents, it's Cameron Quick. I can't believe Lara would let that man back in their lives."

"It's just one night," I added. "That's all we're deciding on now."

Alan threw up his hands. "Fine. We'll discuss it tomorrow evening. Everyone needs to be here for dinner." He looked at my mom. "No overtime."

She nodded and wandered off to their room. I watched her go, knowing our talk was coming soon. I felt it in me, ready to escape. Alan stayed in the kitchen, looking at me hard. "I'm going to check on you in the night," he said. "At random intervals of my choosing."

"I figured."

CHAPTER 19

WE ARE RUNNING THROUGH CAMERON'S YARD, DEAD LEAVES at our feet.

My hand, stinging, is in his.

As we round the corner of the house, toward the driveway, I see the boots first.

I knew it. In one lunge, Cameron's father has him by the arm and his hand is yanked from mine. His father's face is red. *You ruined that window screen.*

I stop running, too, even though I could easily get away now. Cameron's father is shaking him, shaking him hard, and his yelling gets louder and louder and more words come faster and stuck together.

. . . what were you thinking? You are going to pay for it you can count on that.

He looks at me. Still dragging Cameron with one arm he reaches his other for me, close enough that I feel the air near my body move. He reaches for me again; I step away.

And Cameron, for the first time since this began, says something to his father, screams it: *Leave her alone! Leave her alone!*

He screams it so loud that a lady in the house next door sticks her head out a window to see what's going on and tells Cameron's father to *Shut the **** up or I'm going to call the cops again. Why the hell can't you leave those poor children alone for once?*

Cameron's dad lets go of his arm. Cameron, who has been pulling so hard to get away, falls down. His dad leans over and looks into Cameron's face, talking low so that the lady can't hear but I can, *You are going to pay.*

Then he stares at me, long and hard, a slow smile spreading on his face. *Better run home before certain nosy neighbors stop watching and I change my mind about letting you go.*

And I do, all the way home, choking on tears. And I get inside the apartment and Mom is still at work and I wash the blood off my hands and eat the cookies and the Milky Way and some honey. And when she gets home I want to curl in a ball in her lap, but she is running late and throwing her work clothes off to put on her scrubs for school and asking me about my day but asking it quick so that there's no time for real answers.

How was your day, kiddo? Mine was, hah, a challenge, to say the least. Can you heat yourself up some soup for dinner? Good. I'm so sorry, sweetheart, about this. Tomorrow — no, I guess the day after tomorrow — I'll be home all day. Promise.

She pulls me into a hug smelling like grease and pancakes from the Village Inn. I hide my hands in my sweatshirt pockets.

Lock the door and don't answer it for anyone, okay? She kisses the top of my head. *Be good.*

CHAPTER 20

GETTING THE TWO OF US TO SCHOOL WITHOUT ANYONE FIGUR-
ing out that we'd originated from the same house was a challenge.
First, Ethan called, apologetic and begging me to let him give me a
ride to school so we could talk. I told him I was going to work out
with Steph after rehearsal so I needed to have my car.

"She can drive you home from the gym," he said.

"It's out of her way. Also, her driving scares me."

"Okay, but when are we going to talk?"

"Soon." Putting Ethan off wasn't doing either of us any good, and
I knew it, but I just wasn't sure yet exactly what to do about him.

The next problem was finding a way to arrive discreetly without
going to ridiculous lengths like dropping Cameron off a block away
from school or making him wear a disguise or something. "Wouldn't it
be easier to tell the truth?" Cameron asked as we got near Jones Hall.

"No." We pulled into the lot. The coast was clear. "Go ahead," I
said. "I'll see you later, okay?"

"Yep."

Later turned out to be rehearsal — he'd disappeared at lunch and everyone was asking me about him and where he was and how come he never ate lunch with us after that first time, requiring me to believably act like I knew nothing.

When Cameron walked into rehearsal, Ethan said, "Hey, man," and sounded reasonably nice about it. Katy skipped over, her low-rise jeans threatening to fall off her skinny hips. With some girls, that was a sexy look. With Katy, it made you nervous. "Cameron! You're here! Yay."

"Hi."

"Where have you been lately?" She was probably trying to flirt, but it came out a little whiny. "I see you in class but you come in at the last minute and leave the second the bell rings."

"Nowhere."

"How about during lunch and stuff?"

"Library."

"The library!" Her voice was loud. "We are *much* more interesting than the library!" She looked at me for help. "Right, Jenna?"

Bingry walked in with a cup of coffee. "Ethan — get these people off book. Jenna? Is this your whole crew?"

"Freshman Dave is supposed to be here, too." I'd managed to talk him into it at lunch with reminders that it meant hours and hours of extra time hanging out in the same vicinity as Steph.

"He'll have to find us backstage," Bingry said, "Follow me."

Cameron trailed behind as we trekked to the cafetorium/auditeria/gym where we'd actually be putting on the play. There was a storage room underneath the stage, filled with old set pieces and props and a giant pile of used lumber.

"It's all sort of coming back to me now," I said, surveying the junk and remembering the hours spent building the previous year's set for *The Mousetrap.* "How much work we have to do, I mean."

Bingry pulled a sketch out of his pocket. "Good. We can recycle some of this stuff, but we'll need three or four more soft flats, ten feet high, four feet wide. Make sure you frame them up right the first time. Go to it."

He left, and Cameron started pulling the best pieces of wood out of the pile.

"Do you really spend lunch in the library?" I asked, pulling my hair back.

"Yep."

"You can eat with us anytime, you know."

"I know." He made a bunch of noise rummaging in the tool bin. "I still can't believe those crackheads at my old apartment took my tools. It's almost a grand worth of tools and they probably sold them for fifty bucks." He pulled out a drill and looked at it with disgust. "These tools are crap."

"It's just a school play. I don't think it really matters."

"It matters if you want to do something right." His jaw was set, aggravation showing in the tilt of his eyebrows.

"What is it?" I asked.

"My stuff, Jennifer. It's gone. All that's left are some clothes and a few pictures. I had two pots, some dishes, books. I'm not like you; I can't just call my parents and say I need new stuff." He kicked a stack of half-empty paint cans. They clattered to the cement floor. "How am I supposed to make a living without my tools?"

I wanted to reach out and touch his arm, his back, say it was going to be all right, but there in the dusty, quiet underbelly of the stage the world suddenly felt very small. Touching him might not be the best idea.

Someone made a lot of conspicuous noise outside the storage room door; it was Freshman Dave, looking nervous and small. "Oh," he said, "hi. I, um, it took me awhile to find you."

"That's okay," I said. "We haven't really started."

Cameron showed him what to do and we worked in silence until Katy and Steph came to tell us rehearsal was over.

"You're kind of filthy," Steph said, looking me up and down.

I brushed the dust off my pants. "That's what happens when you work."

"Acting is work."

"Okay."

"Are we still going to the gym, or did you exhaust yourself?"

"We're going." It was, after all, my excuse for not carpooling with Ethan.

Cameron kept working, pulling nails out of wood so that we could reuse it. He'd stripped down to his white undershirt; Katy stared at the muscles in his arms, transfixed. Steph was sneaking a few glances herself. "So, Cam," Katy squeaked, "do you need a ride home?"

He looked at me for guidance. When he realized I was going to continue pretending that our plans were completely unconnected, he said, "Sure. Thanks." I wondered where he'd tell her to go.

"See you tomorrow, Jenna," he said, tossing a hammer onto the floor.

"You were slacking in class," Steph said, digging in her locker for hair stuff. "You don't get results unless you really concentrate, you know."

"Yeah, I know." My Pilates form was the least of my worries. I'd spent most of the class imagining Katy and Cameron driving around in her dad's Volvo, her giving him the third degree about his life and the one-word answers he'd probably give and how she'd come to me later for more advice on getting him interested in her.

"So what's the deal with you and Ethan?" Steph rubbed some expensive-looking cream into her hair. "I could totally cut the tension with a knife at lunch. And you didn't talk at rehearsal, either."

I sat on a locker room bench, deciding how much to say. As Jenna Vaughn, I didn't like to have other people know my business, especially when it was something embarrassing like having a stupid fight with my boyfriend. But I had enough secrets to deal with.

"We kind of had a fight last night."

"Seriously? You guys hardly ever fight!"

"He called me a moody bitch."

She dropped her jaw in big, stagy surprise.

"Yeah," I said.

"Were you? A moody bitch?"

"Sort of."

An old lady walked right by us, naked, wrinkled and sagging and perfectly content with herself. We stopped talking until she passed by.

"You know what you guys need? Is to have some fun. We all do. It's senior year, and we haven't had any kind of fun since school started." She pulled on a snug fleece top. "Halloween party. My house. Costumes, candy, horror movies."

I shrugged.

"You shrug? You shrug at my awesome party idea?" She closed her locker much harder than necessary. "Are you going to change, or just wear your gross, sweaty clothes all the way home?"

"Um . . . the second one?" Only after I said it did I realize that in the past, even a few months ago, I might have taken Steph's comment about my gross, sweaty clothes as something mean and personal, the kind of thing people said to Jennifer Harris. I'd changed more than I thought.

We walked out to the parking lot, where the previously sunny sky was now filled with dark clouds. "I bet you anything it's going to snow tonight," I said.

Steph turned on me suddenly. "Are you and Ethan breaking up?"

"I don't know," I said. "We haven't had a chance to talk since last night."

"I mean, I know he can be a pain. And if you don't care about him and you want to be with Cameron, you should. Just go *be* with Cameron and don't make it into such a drama."

161

"Easy for you to say, Steph. You've never not had a boyfriend. I don't know if I want to spend the rest of my senior year single. Anyway, I *do* care about Ethan."

"Listen to what you just said. 'I don't want to be single' is a lot different than 'Wow, I'm crazy about my boyfriend.' And you care *more* about Cameron," she said. "You care more about Cameron than you do about any of us, more than you care about school or the play or our whole four years of high school put together. I can just tell." She threw her gym bag into the trunk of her car. "And it's weird. Because you didn't see him for, what, eight years? And he's been back barely a week? What is it with you two?"

"I . . . don't know," I said.

"Really. I think you do. I had a lot of little boyfriends in grade school and if one came back now I doubt I'd even recognize him," she said. "No one is that loyal to a childhood friend unless he was, like, the love of your life."

"Or your only friend. Or if you went through something together that no one else would understand."

She tilted her head. "Yeahhh. Didn't think of that. My point is, why deny yourself something you really want? I never do."

"It's not that simple. Anyway," I said, smiling, trying to lighten the mood, "you *like* the drama."

"This is true. I have to enjoy it while I can." She slammed her trunk shut. "And you know what I enjoy? Things like a stupid Halloween party or seeing my friends with whatever boy or girl they want. If you want Ethan, have Ethan. If you want Cameron, have him. If it's someone else, great. But don't stay with Ethan just because you're afraid of letting people down." She looked at me and pulled the hood of my sweatshirt up, tucking my hair in to protect it from the drops of rain that had started to fall. "I know you, Jenna. You're the type of girl who would go all the way to the altar with a guy who wasn't right if you thought it would make everyone happy."

The rain came down harder; Steph got in her car and waved as she pulled out, while I stood there, stunned. Not by the suggestion that I should break up with Ethan or be with Cameron or any of that, but that Steph was right — she knew me. Maybe they all *really* did know me. Maybe what Ethan said was right: *You're here now, and you're you.*

"I don't understand, Jenna, why you couldn't give him a ride home?" Mom struck the archetypal Mom pose — hands on hips, perplexed look on face, head tilted at that *I cannot believe you came from my womb* angle. "He walked home in the pouring rain. With a cold, I might add."

"I didn't know he had a cold. I was at the JCC with Steph," I said, knowing that was not going to fly. Cameron padded into the kitchen on bare feet, rubbing his hair dry with a towel.

"It's fine," he said. "I didn't have to walk that far."

Mom shook her head. "It's not fine. While you're living with us, you're part of the family, and we don't leave each other stranded in the rain."

My face got hot. We don't leave each other stranded in the rain,

I thought. We just leave each other home alone every day after school for years. We just lie about terrible things that happen. We just pretend like there's nothing wrong. "You make it sound so uncomplicated, Mom. It's not."

"It really is." She grabbed her purse off the counter. "I have to run to Smith's for a few things for dinner, and when Alan gets home we'll talk. You two figure something out so that this doesn't happen again."

As soon as she left, Cameron said, "She's kind of protective."

"Of you, yeah."

"What does that mean?"

"Nothing." Just that my mother, who didn't even know her nine-year-old was getting terrorized and narrowly missing something much worse, was worried over a big, strong seventeen-year-old's cold. "Where did Katy drop you off?"

"Hardware store on 400 South. I told her I had to get some stuff for the play. She really wanted to wait."

"How'd you talk her out of it?"

He shrugged. "Just told her not to."

I imagined how *that* went over with Katy. As I drew myself a glass of tap water, I caught a glimpse of Cam's big hand closing around a coffee cup. I stopped and I stared. It had been a few days since I'd felt the wonder of it — that this was Cameron Quick, the first boy who ever loved me. And he was alive and standing in my kitchen with bare feet and rain-damp hair and the house was quiet and we were alone.

Like earlier in the under-stage storeroom, I wanted to touch him.

But now, being the only ones in the house and being nearly grown-ups, it would be problematic. For so many reasons.

"Hey," I said. "Sorry about your stuff and everything. I know Alan would be glad to help you get some new tools if you want."

"I'll be okay. Always am."

"I know you are. But people care about you. And would help. If you asked."

"It's hard."

"I understand," I said, running my finger along the counter. "I still haven't told my mom about what happened. That day."

He looked at me, taken aback. "She doesn't know about that?"

I shook my head.

"I thought she knew everything."

"Hardly anything, actually."

"She should. She should know." He set his cup down. "Tell her tonight. Promise me."

He was right; it was time. Past time. I nodded. "I promise."

CHAPTER 21

MY MOTHER HAD GONE INTO FULL-ON HOMEMAKER MODE, working mom version: a roasted chicken from the grocery store, mashed potatoes from the deli, fancy salad, sautéed zucchini with lemon zest. "It's a special night," she said, lighting the candles we usually only pulled out for holidays. "It's a sort of reunion, really, for Jenna and Cameron."

Alan looked skeptical. I wondered how much Mom had really listened to his opinion, if at all. "Where is he now?"

"He was on his way out when I came in from the store," she said. "Just running something down to the mailbox. I still can't get over how *tall* he is. Jenna, honey, would you get the water glasses and fill them?"

I brought out our usual glasses and started to put them on the table. "Oh, not those," Mom said. "The others, from the top shelf?"

We hadn't set the table this nice in ages. Not even for their anniversary. I almost pointed this out but decided against it. Alan and I were mere observers here, watching Mom fulfill some kind of idea she had about what this night was going to be. We helped her set out the food and arrange the silverware. Everything was ready, but Cameron had not come back from the mailbox.

"I'll just look down the street," Mom said, wiping her hands on a kitchen towel. "He's probably headed up the hill."

He wasn't.

Alan picked up a piece of zucchini with his fingers and popped it in his mouth. Mom shot him a look. "I'm sorry," he said, "but I'm starving. Everything looks beautiful. Let's go ahead and enjoy it while it's hot. We can save a plate for Cam."

"Yeah, Mom," I said. "Me, too. Starving."

"Well . . ." She glanced toward the door again. "All right."

We ate. Alan talked about his day but it was clear Mom was not paying attention, throwing in "mm" and "oh" and "ha-ha" absently. Finally she said, "I'm officially worried. Where is he? The mailbox is only three blocks away. Let's call him."

I got up to get my phone and called him, even though I knew he wouldn't answer.

"Maybe we should go out in the car and look," Mom said when I came back.

"Evidently he's taken care of himself for a while now," Alan said. "Maybe he just decided that he doesn't want to stay here after all but didn't have the heart to tell us face-to-face."

"He does this," I said.

Mom set her wine down. "Does what?"

"Disappears. Doesn't communicate. Turns himself off and on."

"Given his childhood," she said, "that's understandable. It's probably a survival mechanism. All the more reason we should show him

167

we care. Probably no one ever went after him. That's what he needs."

I pushed some chicken around on my plate. "I never do that," I muttered.

"Hm?"

"I said I never do that. I'm reliable. I show up for things. I'm where I say I'll be."

Alan nodded as he reached for more potatoes. "True."

"Sweetie," Mom said, "those are wonderful traits. But you had the opportunity to develop those and Cameron did not."

I put my fork down. "I had the 'opportunity to develop' those things? How'd I do that? Waiting around for you to come home from school or work? Having to do my own laundry so the kids didn't tell me I stank?"

She froze in surprise.

"How come you decided to go to nursing school while I was still so young?" I asked. "Why didn't you just wait?"

"What's gotten into you, Jenna? Where is this coming from?"

"Honey," Alan started, then lost momentum and got quiet again.

"I just wonder," I said. "I mean, you're all concerned about Cameron and how he deals with his past. What about me?"

"Jenna," she said, sounding surprised that this still mattered, that I hadn't somehow gotten over it. "I know. I'm sorry. You're right. I could have been home more. I knew that the sooner I got some real job skills, the sooner I could have an actual career with regular hours and benefits and security. And look how it worked out! You've got lots of friends and a boyfriend. You've got a wonderful stepfather who loves you very much. You're happy. Nothing horrible happened and we got through it."

This version of our lives, her version, was important to her. I knew that. It was the story she always told her friends, the one she had probably told Alan when they were dating. I'd heard and overheard it a million times myself:

I was a young mother, didn't know much about the world, and my husband left me. Never sent any child support, nothing, but I decided I wasn't going to spend my life and my energy chasing him down or trying to change him when the only thing I could control was me. I took destiny in my own hands. Waited tables, put myself through nursing school, all while raising a daughter on my own. But she was a trouper and I never gave up and between us we got through it and look at us now! I'm glad things happened the way they did. Everything works out for the best.

And it was a true enough version in some ways. Nothing about it was patently false. It just wasn't the whole story. I felt Alan watching me. "Jenna?" he prompted. "You look like you want to say something."

I glanced at him, could hardly look at my mom. "Something did happen. To me. And Cameron. Something kind of horrible."

She looked stricken and said nothing, like she was afraid to ask what it was. So I kept talking.

• • •

169

The candles had burned nearly down to nubs. I'd played with the wax as it spilled out onto the tablecloth. Mom had cried, as I knew she would, but now she was only angry. Enraged. "Oh, my God, Jenna. Oh, my *God*. Why didn't you *say* something?"

"I don't know."

"I would have gone and personally torn that man's throat out!" Her hand was curled into a fist.

"I don't think so," I said, remembering vividly how tall and scary Cameron's dad was.

"Are you telling me the whole story now? You're not sugarcoating it for me, are you? To spare me the guilt? He didn't . . ." She couldn't say it, whatever she was thinking.

"No. That's it. We got away. Well, I got away."

"It's incredible," Alan said, "the way you were able to think so fast and figure out how to get out of there. Smart girl. Brave girl."

"It was bad enough," Mom said. "Psychological abuse is what it was. And imagine Cameron living with it every day. Every day." She looked at her watch. "We should go out in the car now and look for him. Let's all go together."

Alan answered first. "Absolutely not."

Mom was appalled. "Why not?"

"Because this is not about him right now," he said, adamant. "Think about what your daughter just told you. You're not going anywhere. If Cameron is telling the truth about his legal status then we have no responsibility to him. If he's lying, we still have no responsibility to him and should probably stay away from the situation until we know much, much more. We do, however, have a responsibility to Jenna. Who is sitting right here in front of us," he looked at me. "And we haven't even asked her whether or not she *wants* us to take Cameron in. And honey," he said to Mom, "you can't go back in time and undo it all. No matter how much you want to."

She wiped away more tears. "You're right, I know. I'm just so . . . I feel like the worst mother in the world. And if I let Cameron slip away am I making the same mistake all over again?"

"You're not," I said.

"He's seventeen," Alan reminded her, before turning to me. "What do you think? What do you want to do about Cameron?"

Somehow I'd gotten through my whole story without crying, but now the tears started. "I don't know," I said.

CHAPTER 22

CAMERON WAS RIGHT THERE IN HOMEROOM, ON TIME AND AT his desk. Normally I ignored him in class or pretended to, so as not to worry Ethan or make Katy jealous, but I went over to him to say hi. I knew Ethan was watching. "I told her," I whispered.

"Good. I left so you would. Didn't want to be in the way."

"You could have told us you were leaving."

He shrugged. "Guess I'm not used to that, people caring when I come and go."

"Well, they do."

I noticed Katy gesturing wildly for me to come over to her. "I'm sure you got the word," she said, "about Steph's Halloween party. We're doing it on the actual night of Halloween, even though it's a school night, because it will be so much cooler." She lowered her voice, "And I want to dress in a sexy costume so you *have* to make sure Cameron comes, okay? You *have* to."

"I don't even know if I'm going," I said.

"What?" she screeched. People looked at us. She lowered her

voice again. "Ethan already said he's going to be a pirate and you're going to be his wench. I heard him tell Steph!"

"Well he didn't tell *me*."

At this, Katy stared for a few seconds and then slumped back in her seat. Mr. Moran came in and started calling roll.

I took my lunch to the library, hoping to find Cameron and avoid everyone else. He wasn't there. I sat at a table near the corner and made a barrier with my backpack so I wouldn't get in trouble for eating, then took out my half sandwich, yogurt, and apple, and down at the bottom of my bag, with my napkin, was a piece of paper folded into a small square. My heart pounded and I looked around, wondering how Cameron had gotten to my lunch bag. But when I opened the note, it wasn't from him.

Jennifer-Jenna Elaine Harris Vaughn,

I hope you are having a wonderful day at school!!!

Love,

Mom

It was the kind of note other kids got all the time when they were little, but I never had. I smiled at it, then ate my lunch.

Ethan stood outside Mr. Bingry's room, waiting for me before rehearsal. He looked sulky and irritated. "Where were you at lunch?" he asked.

"I went to the library."

"How come you didn't return my calls yesterday?"

Steph slid by us into the room. "Don't mind me."

After she passed, I said, "Because we were having a family crisis."

"*Your* family had a crisis?"

"Yes, Ethan. My family. Had a crisis. A crisis was had by my family."

"So why were you avoiding me today?"

"I wasn't avoiding you. I was in homeroom, I was in physiology, I was in drama. I don't remember you talking to me then."

He pointed his finger to his chest. "*I'm* the one who wanted to talk about it yesterday. I tried and tried."

More people were coming in to rehearsal. I pulled Ethan away from the door. "I told you: Yesterday was bad."

"Or maybe you're just busy with someone else."

Technically he was right. But not in the way he thought. "Apparently you're not *that* mad," I said, changing the subject, "or else you wouldn't be volunteering me to go to Steph's party and be your wench."

And then Bingry stuck his head out the door. "Ethan, we need to start."

"Sorry. Coming."

"I'll be in the workshop," I said to both of them, "if anyone needs me."

• • •

Cameron was there, working by himself, knee resting on a piece of one-by-four as he framed up a flat. He stopped moving for a second when I walked in and then immediately went back to it, brow knit in concentration. I opened the corner cabinet to start inventorying small props and checking them against the list I had for the play.

"Where'd you sleep last night?" I asked.

"In here. There's a gate behind the cafeteria." He gestured over his shoulder. "Where they put the garbage and stuff. It's easy to climb, and then you just jimmy the window lock and you're in."

"Well, great. That sounds much nicer than my parents' sofa."

"Can you hold this crosspiece?" he asked. I knelt next to him, steadying the shorter length of wood while he checked it. "It's gotta be a perfect ninety-degree angle. That's what Bingry meant when he said frame it up right."

"Oh."

"I'm not your problem, Jenna," he said quietly. "I don't ever want to be your problem. Or your family's."

I didn't know what to say. I couldn't exactly deny he'd been a problem in some ways. I just kept holding the wood while he took some screws out of a can on the floor. "I should have protected you that day," he said, quieter still. "You shouldn't have had to be the one to get us out of there. It should have been me to stand up to him."

"You did," I said, "in the end. You did your best."

"You don't need to go saving me all over again." He connected the two pieces of wood with the electric screwdriver, which made a high, whining sound. We didn't notice Freshman Dave come in until

Cameron turned the screwdriver off. "You really have trouble finding this place," Cameron said to Dave.

"Um, yeah." The truth was he was probably watching rehearsal as long as he could without being conspicuous, hoping that Steph would even glance his way.

"Here," Cam said, handing Dave the screwdriver. "You do the other end. I'll hold it."

I let go, stood up. They talked and built while I looked for a soup ladle, a pack of cards, a spray can. We didn't have them, or anything else on my prop list. I didn't know why I was doing this, anyway, when what I really needed was to spend more time trying to pass trig. Well, I did know. I was doing it for Ethan because I thought that was part of what a good girlfriend did, and I'd spent all of junior high and high school observing those around me to see what "normal" looked like. I'd tried to learn it from the outside in.

I looked at my hand resting on the shelf of the prop cabinet, thinking of the scars that were there whether anyone could see them or not.

"Hey, Freshman Dave," I said.

"Yeah?" He stood up, all five feet of him, and stared behind my head.

"How would you feel about being stage manager?"

Cameron watched me.

"Oh," Dave said, horrified, "no. No. That's an important job."

"I know." I handed him my clipboard. "You might have to go to the dollar store for some of this stuff. And while you're there, get Steph a bag of salt and vinegar chips. She'll do anything for those."

I left the workroom and went to see Miss Betts to tell her I needed extra help with trig.

When I got home, Alan was already there. I found him in the back-yard, crouched among the white and yellow mums. There was a tiny, fresh mound of dirt at his feet. "We lost Estella last night," Alan said, tidying the dirt with his spade. "I guess I knew it was coming."

"Sorry," I said. "Hopefully she didn't suffer."

"I know they're just fish, but it gets me every time." He stood up. "I need a snack."

We went through the kitchen cabinets until I retrieved a box of crackers and jar of peanut butter. A few minutes later we both stood at the counter, me smearing blobs of peanut butter onto crackers and handing them to him or eating them myself, sharing a glass of milk.

"I ran into the dean of the English department yesterday," he said as soon as he could talk. "She told me that you're welcome to stop by anytime if you want to talk about your application essay or any-thing else."

"Oh. Thanks." Sometimes the idea of college snuck up on me. Cameron wouldn't be the only one out in the world on his own; we all would. Except I always knew I had a home to come to anytime I needed it. I turned to Alan, who was sucking peanut butter off his teeth. "Do you ever feel helpless?"

"Helpless, useless, clueless. And old. Don't forget old."

"He said I didn't need to save him."

"But you want to."

"Yeah. But I can't. Right?"

"Probably not. Usually not."

I called Ethan that night. He answered, and I could tell he was out somewhere and not at home. "Are you driving?" I asked. "I can call later."

"It's okay. Gil's driving."

"Oh. Where're you guys going?"

"I don't know. Just cruising up State Street now . . ."

I could hear laughter, people talking, a car radio. "Just you and Gil?"

"Um, Katy is here, too. And Jill." Jill Stevenson, from the play. So, Ethan, Gil, Katy, and Jill. A perfect boy-girl ratio. "We're just —"

"Jenna?" It was Katy. She must have grabbed the phone. "We were going to call you but Ethan said you had family stuff and anyway you were gone after rehearsal. Freshman Dave said you made him stage manager? What the hell?"

"I don't have time. I'm going to flunk trig."

There was a thumping sound, and a screech of laughter. Then Ethan was back on the line, breathless. "Sorry. Katy totally dropped the phone. Klutz!"

"I better go," I said, trying very hard to keep my voice even.

"I'll call you when I get home."

"Ethan . . . Let's talk Monday, okay? Give me the weekend off."

There was a long pause. The background noise got quieter. "If you want."

"I do."

"Well. Bye."

I started to say bye but he'd already hung up.

CHAPTER 23

ON SUNDAY AFTERNOON, MOM AND I WERE PLAYING SCRABBLE
at the kitchen table since I had actually, for once, finished my homework by Saturday night. She was asking me about Ethan and why I
hadn't been out over the weekend. My habit was to not tell her anything of any significance, but we were attempting to forge new wa-
ters. Ever since I'd told her about what had happened with Cameron's
dad, she'd given me a lot of long looks but hadn't said much. I knew
she felt guilty — for not being there, for not having even a clue that
something that horrifying had happened to me. It made her act dif-
ferently around me. Quieter, but also solicitous and available. Like
she had to win me back.

To show that I wanted things to be different, too, I actually told
her the truth.

"I think maybe Ethan and I broke up," I said, arranging my Scrabble tiles in front of me: YELP. LEAP. FLAY. FLEA.

Her face fell. "What happened?"

"I'm not sure, actually." I placed my word across one of hers:

FLAYED. "We might not be broken up. I think it's up to me, and I have to decide."

"Well." She looked down at her letters. "Does all this have anything to do with Cameron coming back?"

"Basically."

She didn't put any letters down. Our game had effectively stopped. "I know you might think you want to be with Cameron that way," she said, "but remember it's been such a short time that he's been back, and —"

"It's not that."

"Are you sure?"

"I don't picture us together, like a couple. It's more like . . ."

"Like a brother?"

"Mom, could you just listen?" She clamped her lips shut. "Not like a brother," I said. "It's almost like nothing would be enough. Being a couple wouldn't be enough. Being like brother and sister wouldn't be enough. It's an endless sense of . . . I don't know." I could tell it was killing her to not talk. I sighed. "Go ahead."

"Unfinished business," she said, with a rush of breath. "That's what I see between you two."

"Unfinished business?"

"Yes. And I think it will feel that way until the day you die."

I looked at her to see if she was serious. She was. "Great."

The doorbell rang during dinner. Alan got up to answer, saying, "If it's the missionaries I might let them in. I'm too tired to put up a fight."

It wasn't missionaries. It was Cameron.

He and Alan walked into the kitchen together. "He's sick," Alan said.

"Hi," he said weakly, meeting my eyes for the briefest second.

"What is it?" Mom asked, getting up and shifting into nurse mode. "Did you walk here? Sit down. Tell me what you're feeling."

"Throat aches. Head aches. Everything aches."

He sank into a chair at the table. Mom put her hand to his forehead. "You've definitely got a fever. When did this start?"

"My cold got better, but it kind of turned into this last night. I thought I'd feel better this morning but I feel worse. Didn't know where to go."

"You know you're welcome here," Mom said. She looked to me, then Alan. "Right?"

"Right," I said. Alan nodded.

She turned her focus back to Cameron. "Have you eaten anything today?"

He shook his head.

"Jenna will fix you a plate while I set you up on the couch."

"How about the sofa bed in my study?" Alan asked. "It should be warmer in there."

"Good idea. Come on." She helped Cameron up and led him out of the kitchen.

Alan got a plate out of the cupboard and handed it to me. "Is this okay with you, Jenna? For him to stay here?"

"Yeah," I said. "It's good. You have no idea what it takes for him to ask for help."

I spent all evening in Alan's office, reading at his desk and keeping Cameron company. Mostly he slept, snoring lightly and once in a while murmuring unintelligible somethings into his pillow. I turned my chair so that I could look at him whenever I wanted, at his face or at the bare foot that stuck out from under the covers, or at his arm dangling off the side of the sofa bed.

Around eleven, when I was ready for bed, Cameron woke up. I brought him broth and crackers. "Hi," I said.

"Have you been here all this time?"

"Most of it."

Alan's beige pajamas looked small and uncomfortable on Cameron. "You don't have to," he said. "I can take care of myself." He reached for the broth. I watched him slurp straight from his bowl, everything about him becoming younger and more boyish by the second — rosy lips on the white rim of the bowl, wrists without enough pajama sleeve to cover them, cowlick hair and sleepy eyes.

"I know you can. But you don't have to."

"Well . . ." He finally looked at me. "Thanks."

Monday was the day of reckoning for me and Ethan. I knew we were breaking up, I just hadn't figured out how exactly to do it, no plan for what to say. He, apparently, had a very clear plan. He was waiting by my locker, a smile on his face, expecting a hug. Which I gave him, out of habit.

"J.V., I missed you," he said. "Your break is officially over, okay? I didn't like it. I'm sorry for what I said about you being a moody bitch. I'm sorry I volunteered you for stage manager without asking. Sorry for being a jerk and everything. Don't be mad at me anymore. I hate it."

What about going out Friday without me? With Jill instead? I thought it but didn't ask. The school hallway was not the right place for the conversation we needed to have. "So Freshman Dave is going to stage manage," I said. "That's okay?"

"Yep. And you are going to pass trig."

"Promise?"

"There are no guarantees in life, Jenna."

I tried to laugh. "If you only knew how true that is."

The discussion at lunch centered on the Halloween party. Steph had big plans. "We're going to trick-or-treat," she said. "I don't care how old we are. We are going to exploit the free candy situation to its maximum potential because it might be our last chance, ever."

Katy groaned. "Really? Trick-or-treating? I heard it might snow."

"So?" She'd already gotten half a dozen horror movies from the video store, laid in a supply of junk food, and, she now said in a dramatic stage whisper, "Booze."

Gil rolled his eyes. "This is Jones Hall, not East High. We don't *drink*. We never have before. Why start now?"

"Well, that's the point," Ethan said. "There are no dances at Jones. No real sports — sorry, Katy, I don't count tennis. We should experience *something* authentically teenagery while we're still actual teenagers."

"Jenna?" Steph asked. "Opinion?"

My opinion was that Ethan's rationale was lame. What I said: "If I got caught my parents would literally kill me, so I won't be drinking. But as long as there is no drunk driving or drunk sex or drunk fights, I don't really care what anyone else does."

"Will Cameron drink?" Katy asked. "Where is he, anyway?"

"I haven't seen him."

"Does that dude ever come to school?" Gil asked. "He's in some of my classes, or so I've heard."

"He's pretty smart," I said. "Maybe he's bored with class."

"We're *all* bored with class. All I know is, if it were me? My mom would be all over my butt if I missed ten minutes of school."

"Not everyone has a mother."

Katy laughed, thinking I was making a joke. "Jenna, you're so funny."

My mom and Cameron were sitting at the kitchen table when I got home, playing a game of backgammon. There was a plate on the table with half of what looked like a homemade cookie left, and milk-filmed glasses. Some sort of soup or stew simmered on the stove.

"Oh, there you are," Mom said.

Cameron lifted a couple of fingers. "Hi."

"What are you doing home?" I asked my mom.

"Well, I got to work and we were a tiny bit overstaffed on the floor, so I asked if I could come home at noon." She smiled, radiant and maternal and beaming the kind of pride moms get when they bake cookies and make homemade soup. "I thought Cameron might like some company."

I honestly could not remember one time when my mom took off work or missed class or came home early to take care of me, other than the day I fainted at school, the day I thought Cameron died. If I had a cold, she'd leave a box of cold medicine and some cans of chicken noodle on the counter and remind me to get plenty of fluids. The few times I was sicker than that, she paid the babysitter for extra hours.

"That's nice," I said.

Mom picked up the leftover half cookie and ate it. "Dinner might be later than usual," she said. "I think we spoiled our appetites."

"I'm starving."

"Oh," she said distractedly, studying the backgammon board. "You can fix yourself a snack, hm?" Cameron rolled his dice; Mom grimaced. "That's your third doubles in a row. It's hardly fair."

"Yeah," I said, "I'll just fix myself a snack." I found a package of Fig Newtons and took it to my room with what was left of the milk. I ate four, five, and half of a sixth, then stopped. If I kept going, which I could have easily done, I'd spend the rest of the night feeling sick and then be cranky and emotional in the morning, again, and what was it really giving me, all this eating? Tight clothes was what. What did I want? What did I really want?

I called Ethan, ready to break the news. "How was rehearsal?" I asked.

"Better."

"We should probably talk."

"I won't drink at the party," he said quickly. "If you don't want me to, I won't. I swear it right now. My hand is on a stack of Bibles."

I paused. "That's very chivalrous."

"Chivalrous would be my middle name, if I could spell it."

"Ethan . . ."

"Jenna?"

It was hard to break up with someone who never let you get around to it. "My mom is calling me," I lied. "I'll talk to you later."

Cameron was quiet at dinner, when we finally ate. He looked and sounded a lot healthier than he had the night before but kept his head down and only answered direct questions. "Are you coming back to school tomorrow?" I asked.

"Probably."

"That's a good start," Alan said, biting into his corn bread, sending a cascade of yellow crumbs down the front of his blue shirt. "Then what's your plan?"

Mom looked pointedly at Alan. "Not that there's any pressure for him to have a plan."

Alan opened his mouth to say something, then closed it and picked up his wine and sort of raised his eyebrows. I smashed a piece of tomato against the side of my bowl. "You can't live in the prop room until graduation," I said.

"I won't be here that long," Cameron said, avoiding my eyes. "I'm going back to California."

"What?" Mom looked from Cameron to Alan to me and back to

187

Cameron. "Cam, honey, think about this. You should graduate. We'll work something out. Maybe you'll get a job and find another place. The cost of living here is so much lower than in California."

I stared at Cameron but he still wouldn't look at me. "I need to be closer to my brothers and sisters," he said.

My mind had stopped at "going back to California." He'd just gotten here. I'd just started to understand him, us, a tiny bit.

". . . think about the good you can do them if you have a diploma," Mom was saying. "Jones Hall is such a good school for you."

"I want to see if I can file for custody, maybe," Cameron said. "I need to get back to them."

"All the more reason to finish school. It will give you a much stronger case."

"Mom," I said. "He doesn't want to stay. He wants to go back." Not that I was happy about it, but I knew there wasn't much point in trying to talk him out of something he really wanted to do. The boy had determination. He had determined that he'd come to Utah and find me, and now he'd determined it was time to leave.

"I'm just saying that he should really think it through. . . ." She was near tears. Alan reached over and patted her hand. "Honey," he whispered. "It's okay."

I glanced at Cameron. He looked down at his food. We all sat like that a long time.

• • •

188

I woke in the night. The chill in my room, the quiet, the eerie light coming through the window — it all said snow. I got up and pulled on an extra sweatshirt, moving down the hall toward Alan's study. The door was ajar a couple of inches; I pushed it open. "Cameron? Cam?"

"I'm awake."

"Get up," I whispered. "I want to show you something."

His silhouette rose and came to me.

"Put on your coat and shoes."

He did.

I took his hand and led him back down the hall, past the humming fish tank, through the living room and out the front door. We stepped into the still, cold air. The street and sidewalk, the roof of every house, every car, the power lines, every tiny branch of every tree, had been covered by a neat layer of sparkling snow.

Quiet. Quiet. Nothing untouched by the white. The world and everything in it had changed overnight.

"I haven't seen anything like this since I left Utah," Cameron said.

"Remember that time at my apartment? You raised that blind like you were showing me the eighth wonder of the world."

"I was."

"Usually by the time I wake up, the plows and snowblowers have ruined everything." The muffling effect of the snow made our voices intimate. "Don't worry about my mom," I said. "I think she's trying to make up for other things, you know? If she can take care of you maybe she won't feel so guilty about not being there more when I was growing up."

He stared out into the street. We were still holding hands. His was much bigger than mine, bigger than Ethan's. I felt completely enveloped in it.

"When I was a kid," he said, "I had this doll. A baby doll. Stole it from the play area in kindergarten class."

"Really? You stole it?"

"Yeah. I kept it hidden in this old suitcase in a closet. Not *my* closet. If my dad found it I wanted it to just look like something someone had forgotten a long time ago."

I let my other hand hover over the snow on the porch railing, tempted to leave my handprint then deciding not to.

"I would take the baby out," Cameron continued, "when my dad wasn't home. There was a rocking chair by the living room window. I'd take the baby and rock it. This one time, it was just like this outside. I opened the window because I liked to feel the cold air. Wrapped the baby in a towel, as if it was a blanket."

"You didn't want the baby to get cold."

He smiled. "Right. And I sat in that chair and rocked it and rocked it while I watched the snow."

I sighed, my breath making a white cloud. This was a memory I wanted to keep, whole, and recall again and again. When I was fifty years old I wanted to remember this moment on the porch, holding hands with Cameron while he shared himself with me. I didn't want it to be something on the fringes of my memory like so many other things about Cameron and myself.

190

"When do you think you're leaving?" I asked.

"I don't know. Probably soon. Got what I came here for."

"Even though we didn't go back to your old house?"

"That was only part of it," he said. "Not the main thing."

A few more big flakes of snow drifted down from the starlit sky. "And what was the main thing?"

"This," he said. "Right here."

CHAPTER 24

CAMERON RODE WITH ME TO SCHOOL AND WE STOPPED FOR
donuts and coffee, watching the snow come down in fat flakes. He
told me about his siblings, showing me pictures. "Jake is the oldest,"
he said. "Fourteen and already taller than my dad. He's keeping
things together, making sure the rest of them are okay." He leaned
forward and pointed. "This is Ryan. He's eleven. Lizzie is eight; Bran-
don just turned five."

"Your mom must have been young when she had you." I looked
at picture after picture of kids who looked like smaller versions of
Cameron, dark hair and big eyes. All that time I knew Cam as a kid,
I had no idea there were brothers and sisters. It was weird the way
your world could be so small, like you're looking at life through the
tiniest of peepholes.

"She was my age. Met my dad in high school, got pregnant,
dropped out, married. Then just kept having kids."

"Do they know you're coming back?"

"Gonna call Jake later to check in. I'll tell him then."

"They're lucky," I said. I was already imagining our good-bye — we'd both cry, we'd have a good long hug, we'd say things we might be scared to say if we knew we had to look each other in the eye the next day.

"I don't know about that. I can be a pain." He laughed then, and bit into a donut. "You might have noticed."

I laughed, too. "Might have."

Ethan, waiting at my locker, wore an eye patch, puffy shirt, and raggedy vest. His face fell when we saw me. "You were supposed to be dressed as my wench," he said, staring pointedly at my jeans and sweater.

"It's Halloween," I said. "Today."

"Yes."

"Crap."

"I can't believe you forgot."

"I'm sorry."

"S'okay. I'll just have to be a wenchless pirate." He pulled me into a dramatic, swashbuckling kiss. "Arrrrr!"

"Easy there, matey," I said, pushing him back gently. It didn't seem right to be making out with him when I was planning to execute the breakup within the next twenty-four hours. "We've got a whole day of school ahead of us."

Two freshman girls dressed as Mormon pioneers walked and made hungry, wishful eyes at Ethan. He did look rakish and yummy in his costume, I could see that objectively. But I didn't have any physical or emotional reaction to the fact of him. Which made me sad.

In trig, Katy leaned over, her hair in two sticking-out braids that nearly poked me in the eye. She glanced toward Cameron, who was feeling better and in his seat in the front row. "Has the Great Mysterioso said anything to you about the party?"

"Like what, for instance?" I kept one eye on Miss Betts, who was involved in a lengthy whiteboard explanation with Nicole Threedy.

"That he's coming?" she whispered. "Or not coming? Anything about me? Anything about Steph? *Anything,* Jenna. Anything means anything."

Katy's voice was never as quiet as she believed it to be, and I imagined Cameron could hear our whole conversation. "Not that I remember," I said. "What are you supposed to *be,* anyway?" She had on a white tunic, black leggings, and striped leg warmers.

She slapped her hands on her desk; Miss Betts turned around. "Girls? Is there a question?"

"No, thank you, Miss Betts," Katy said, then lowered her whisper only slightly. "I'm Pippi effing Longstocking! Please don't tell me you thought I was actually dressed like this as *me!*"

"I thought you were going to dress sexy. Anyway, shouldn't you be more patchy than stripy?"

"*I* never read the stupid book. This was all Steph's idea."

Miss Betts stopped writing on the whiteboard but didn't turn around. "Katy. I can still hear you."

"Sorry."

After class, Katy grabbed Cameron as we all shuffled out into the hall. "Hey, how come you didn't dress up?" She meant to make chit-chat, but in traditional Katy style it came out sounding overly urgent, like an accusation.

"I haven't done Halloween since I was nine."

"Come to the party tonight," Katy said, not taking any hint whatsoever from Cameron's flat tone. "I'm sure Jenna told you that we're going out to get what candy we can and then we'll use the sugar to help us stay up all night."

He looked at me.

"I didn't even realize today was Halloween until I got to school," I said. "So, no, I didn't mention it."

Katy straightened her leg warmers. "Well, it's happening. Don't forget."

At lunch, Steph and Gil were absorbed in some sort of complicated plan to acquire alcohol. "We should just get a giant bottle of bargain vodka or something," Gil said, pushing his gorilla mask back on his head.

"Not classy," Steph said. "This is a special night, not a frat party."

"Special? Classy?" Ethan asked. "Steph. We're seniors in high school going trick-or-treating. We look like third-rate street performers."

Katy's eyes were on the cafeteria door. "What is Cameron's problem? I saw him in the hall ten minutes ago and he pretended not to see me. He won't even eat with us. I am so over him. I don't know what I saw in him in the first place."

"Guffaw," Gil said. "You saw he was available."

"Don't give up before you've even started, Katy," Steph said. "You never know what can happen. We can get him drunk and take advantage of him."

Katy laughed. "*We?*"

I didn't have the heart to tell her the chances of him coming were virtually zero. It would take hours to explain the whole situation — his childhood, emancipation, why he was here, why he was going back. And most of all, why he was living with me.

Steph was detailing her master plan: ". . . and then we'll completely beautify Katy and get everyone just the tiniest bit tipsy. Gil will come on to me and we'll act like we suddenly realize we're in love and we'll be all over each other —"

"Gee, Gil," I interrupted, "how'd she get you to agree to *that?*"

"— and Jenna will be with Ethan, leaving Cam horny and drunk with only Katy to play with. Et cetera. Unless anyone wants to swap partners," she said, eyeing me.

"Note how you went from 'the tiniest bit tipsy' to 'horny and drunk,'" I said, playing along even though I knew none of this would ever happen. "That worries me. Just a little."

"Jenna," Steph said in her 'try to keep up with me' voice, "we're seniors. This is, like, a ritual that goes on all over the country. What could go wrong?"

"Um, everything?"

"So negative," she said, shaking her head.

"What time should I pick you up?" Ethan asked. He was ready to go into rehearsal. I knew Cameron was waiting for me at my car and I didn't want to dawdle.

"Maybe I'll meet you there," I said.

"Jenna! Come on, let me just pick you up. It's on the way." He played with my scarf. "Then I can take you home and your parents will be asleep by then and I can come in and stuff."

"Ethan, I —"

Bingry opened the door. "What will it take to get you here on time, Ethan?"

"Sorry." To me: "I'll be there at six. Look sexy."

On the way home, Cameron put his hands on the dashboard, spreading his long fingers, craning his head to look through the windshield and up at the sky. "It's going to snow again. I remember that sky."

Everything outside had gone gray and flat and still. "We've had the first snow before November," I said. "Sign of a long winter." I saw it stretching out in front of me, cold and gloomy with no Cameron and no boyfriend.

"Remember that time we got snowed in at school? Everyone had to wait for their parents to get them, but our parents didn't come."

"God," I said, "I'd forgotten. Why can't I remember any of this stuff without being reminded?"

"School bus driver had to take us home eventually. We were the only two kids on the bus."

"I can picture us," I said, "sitting next to each other on that back-seat. It's such a sad scene, really."

I felt him look at me. "I don't think so. I never thought of it as sad."

"But Cameron, every single kid in the school got picked up by their parents except us!" I was laughing now at the tragic ridiculous-ness of it. "It was pathetic!"

"We had each other. I never needed anyone else. That's the dif-ference between you and me," he said. "You need all these people around you. Your friends, your boyfriend, everyone. Every single person has to like you. I only ever needed that one person. Only ever needed you."

"Not everyone has to like me," I protested. "It's just . . ." We'd ar-rived at my house. "Imagine if you'd believed I died," I said. "Trust me, you'd start to need other people. You had the luxury of always knowing I was alive, knowing where I was and what I was doing. I didn't have that, Cameron."

"I didn't think of it that way when it was happening," he said. "Didn't ever think you needed me much as I needed you."

"I did."

"I'm sorry," he said. "But I knew you'd be okay."

"How, Cameron? How did you know that?"

"Look at you. From the day you marched across the school yard to talk to me," he said, starting to smile a little at the memory, "I knew you were stronger than I'd ever be."

"You're the one who got yourself away from your parents in the long run. You're the one supporting yourself, being an adult."

"Maybe. Hey," he said, teasing, "ain't a competition, anyway. We can both be strong."

I smiled. "Yeah. Good."

I looked in my closet for something suitably wenchlike but couldn't come up with anything. "Look sexy," Ethan had said. I ended up borrowing a pair of my mom's scrubs for my costume.

She made us eat an early dinner so that the diet for the night would not consist entirely of candy. The doorbell kept ringing. After four or five times, Alan stopped answering. "What self-respecting child goes trick-or-treating before dark?"

"I'm just not in the mood," Mom said, taking a gulp of wine. "We should turn out the porch light and lock the doors."

"I'll pass out candy," Cameron said.

Alan got up to clear the dishes. "Don't you want to go out with Jenna and her friends?" he asked.

"No," we both said at the same time. "Also," I said, turning to Cameron sheepishly, "Ethan is picking me up here at six. Maybe you could, like . . ." I made hand gestures of indeterminate meaning.

"He could, like, what?" Mom asked.

"Hide," Cameron said. "Right?"

"Essentially."

Mom did not look happy. "Jenna, have you not told Ethan that Cameron is staying here?"

"Well, no. I haven't."

"Why on earth not?"

"Maybe we should stay out of it," Alan said to my mom.

The bell rang. Cameron jumped up to get it. He walked in with Ethan, who had on his pirate outfit, with his coat over it and the eye patch resting on his forehead. "I guess I'm early," he said. "Sorry." Cameron went over to the stove and ate a couple more bites of food with a serving spoon while Ethan watched.

As soon as I saw Ethan's face, I knew he'd been drinking. His eyes, nervous and unfocused, gave him away. I needed to get him out of there before my parents noticed. "It's okay," I said. "I'm ready."

"What about your costume?"

"This is my costume."

He stared at me in the plain, baggy scrubs, disappointed. "Oh."

"Come on." I turned to my parents. "Bye. I'll be late."

"Be good," Mom said.

As soon as we were out on the porch, I said, "Are you crazy?"

"What?"

"You said you wouldn't drink. You swore."

"Is he coming, or what? Tell him to hurry up."

"Who?"

"Who do you think? Cameron. Your friend."

"No," I said. "He's not coming."

Ethan pointed to the door with an unsteady finger. "Then why is he in your house? You know what he said to me when he got the door? He said I'd better not get you in any trouble or he'd kick my ass. Kick my ass!"

If I wasn't so angry at Ethan, I would have laughed at that. "You swore," I repeated, "that you wouldn't drink."

"Steph made me. I only had a little." He was completely unsorry. "She drove me here. You think I'm gonna drink and drive?" I leaned to look past him and saw Steph's car idling in front of the house. She waved; I didn't wave back. Ethan looked me up and down, making a pouty face. "Your costume sucks."

"Maybe I don't want to be your *wench*, Ethan." Steph beeped the horn. "Let's just go."

CHAPTER 25

"I CAN'T BELIEVE THIS CRAP. JOLLY RANCHERS? GUMMY worms?" Katy rifled through the pile of candy she'd dumped onto Steph's floor. "Where's the chocolate? Where's the candy corn?"

"I *like* Jolly Ranchers," Steph said, helping herself to Katy's rejects, her boobs in danger of breaking loose from her Renaissance dress.

Gil watched, fascinated. "Remind me who you are again?"

"Um, Juliet? From *Romeo and Juliet?*" She popped a candy into her mouth. "Shakespeare?"

"Did they really dress like that back then?" Gil asked. "It seems kind of like something that might get you burned at the stake."

"I'm pre-Puritan, baby."

Ethan unwrapped a peanut butter cup from his own candy pile. "You've obviously never been to a Renaissance fair, dude. I went to one in New York with my cousin? Boobs galore."

"We gotta get one of those in Utah," Gil said.

Our trick-or-treating hadn't lasted long. The snow had stopped falling, but there was plenty on the ground and it was too wet and cold to be trekking around in costumes. Anyway, some people called us on being too old, and we weren't having fun: Gil and Katy were pissed about Cameron not being there; Katy for obvious reasons and Gil because it meant his role in the plan — i.e., groping Steph — was no longer required. Also, Ethan and Steph were tipsy and being obnoxious.

Now, we were in Steph's family room surrounded by candy and the bottle of vodka and nary a parent in sight.

"Are we going to watch a movie or not?" I asked.

Katy emptied a minibox of Nerds into her mouth and asked, "Why doesn't Cameron like us?"

"Yeah," said Gil. "We're likable. Right?"

"He barely knows you," I said.

Katy laughed. "He barely knows *you*, Jenna!"

"Oh, he knows her," Steph said.

Ethan nodded. "He *really* knows her. He's her body guard, too, I found out. Threatened to kick my ass if anything happened to her."

Katy stared straight ahead, Pippi braids drooping and knees drawn to her chest. "I knew it," she said.

"Knew what?" Steph asked.

"Cameron and Jenna. Jenna and Cameron. It's been obvious since the day he showed up."

Gil looked at me. "Okay, I'm officially confused."

"It's simple," Ethan said, taking a swig from the vodka bottle. "Jenna's been cheating on me."

I stared at the carpet. "I have not. You guys have no idea what you're talking about. You don't know anything about the situation."

"Tell us," Katy said.

Steph looked sad. This evening was not going as she'd hoped.

"He's . . ." I shook my head. I could have explained how he was homeless and needed somewhere to stay. How he was wounded and needed someone who understood. How he was a hero, surviving his father and going back to save the others. But none of those things were any of their business, and none of them explained why he mattered to me. "He's the one person who knows everything about me," I finally said. "And loves me anyway."

"So . . ." Gil said, "you *are* cheating on Ethan?"

"Shut up, Gil," Steph muttered.

"Are you saying I don't know you, Jenna?" Ethan looked like he might possibly start to cry, staring at me like he and I were the only ones in the room. "Because what's the point of having a girlfriend if she thinks I don't know her?"

Steph looked almost as upset as Ethan. "What don't we know about you that would make us not love you, Jenna?"

"Yeah," Gil said. "Have a little faith."

"We've been friends for almost four years," Katy added. "Hello, *all* of high school?"

Ethan was still near tears. "If you're going to break up with me, just do it."

I've been trying, I thought, but didn't say it, knowing that would hurt and embarrass him more than anything. "Can we talk about this later?" I asked. "In private?"

"Breakups happen all the time," Steph said. "We'll all survive it." She slopped some vodka into a cup and held it out to me. "Jenna, have a drink. And I'll put on the movie and we'll keep ingesting sugar and things will seem better, you'll see."

"*Seem* better," I said. "But not *be* better." I stood and got my jacket, leaving Steph there holding out the cup. "I'm sorry, Steph. Can someone sober please give me a ride home?"

Alan was still up, surrounded by candy wrappers and watching TV. I fell onto the couch next to him. "Where's Mom?"

"She went to bed early with one of her headaches. Cameron turned in awhile ago, too." He peeked into my plastic bag of candy. "Anything good?"

"I sort of ate all the chocolate stuff."

"Are there any Circus Peanuts?"

"Who likes Circus Peanuts?"

"Me," he said, finding one of the gross peanut-shaped marsh-mallows.

We were quiet awhile, surrounded by only the sounds of un-wrapping and crunching and chewing, and the TV. I gnawed on a Dum Dum stick. "Ethan and I are done," I said finally.

"I'm sorry."

"He was my first boyfriend."

"I know."

"The only real boyfriend I've had. I'm a senior in high school and he was my only real boyfriend."

"I know."

"And I won't find another one at Jones Hall. That is guaranteed."

"Okay."

"This is all very sad and tragic," I said.

Alan unwrapped a sleeve of Smarties. "Yet, oddly, you don't seem that upset."

"I know."

Hours later, I was still awake in bed and worrying over what the rest of my high school life would be like. I was scared to go back to Jones and face them all. Maybe I'd have to eat lunch alone in the library until graduation. Katy might not ever talk to me again. She'd given me a ride home, saying, "I'm only doing this because I don't want to be at the party, either." We didn't talk the rest of the way.

I thought of what Cameron said about the day I came across the yard to him to ask him to be in my club. About how I had guts. About how I was brave and strong. He was around to tell me these things now, to remind me, but I was going to have to learn how to remember them myself, and believe them.

I got up, crept to Alan's office, and went in.

"Cameron? Cam?"

He didn't move, and appeared to be fast asleep.

I'm not sure what I wanted. To look at him, I guess, and talk. I sat on the floor by the sofa bed so that my face was level with his. His breath came in short, toothpaste-minty sighs.

"Cameron Quick," I whispered, just wanting to hear his name. He still didn't move. I touched his face, following the curve of his jaw, the bow of his lips. This was the boy who made my childhood less lonely, who made me feel loved. And known. And accepted. Who had stared into my most terrifying moment right beside me, while my most terrifying moment was his everyday life. And I pictured him patting that baby doll by a cold window, showing it comfort by instinct. I felt overwhelmed with sadness for his life and what it could have been, even though I knew he wouldn't want me to feel that way. He'd say it was all right, that he'd get by, that he could take care of himself. That he didn't need anyone to fix it. But I still wanted to, to somehow make up for that infinite, infinite well of helplessness that I'd spent most of my life believing had swallowed us up.

It hadn't, though, because we were here, weren't we? Wiser and braver and more ready for life than our friends or parents or anyone we knew, than even I had realized until he came back to show me.

I touched his wrist lightly, his elbow. I tucked the blanket up around his shoulder.

"I love you, Cameron," I whispered.

He was gone in the morning. November first, a day I'd forever keep in my mind as a landmark. I was the least surprised of us all. Mom couldn't believe it. "I thought he'd stay until graduation," she said, walking through the house desultorily. "I honestly thought he'd change his mind and stay. Maybe he'll be at school. Maybe he just left early to . . ." Her voice trailed off, sad and quiet.

"His stuff is gone, honey," Alan said.

"He won't be at school," I said. I poured bran flakes into a bowl, covered them in skim milk. I felt numb and had a sugar hangover from the Halloween candy, and half wondered if I'd dreamed going into his room and telling him I loved him. Maybe he'd heard me. Maybe that's what made him leave. I'd scoured my room for a note from him, a message, a sign, anything. I didn't find one.

At school, no one outside our circle really noticed or cared that he wasn't there. His attendance had been so random, anyway, and we were used to people coming and going, trying on the school to see if it fit, parents hoping this would be the place where little Johnny or Susie might finally do something right or at least not get beat up.

Ethan didn't come to school, and Steph made me sit at our usual table even though I'd been on my way to the library with my brown bag, figuring that would be least awkward for everyone. "You can't do that," she said. "I've gone through a million breakups and trust me, you have to immediately make a statement and show you're not going to run off and hide. When Ethan comes back to school, he'll see how it's going to be and he'll just have to deal with it."

"Right," I said. "Okay."

And he did, the next day and the next day and the rest of the year, all of us pressing on to graduation like Cameron had never been there at all.

That didn't stop me from looking for him. For weeks and weeks, I imagined I saw him everywhere. I'd drive down State Street and think it was him standing in front of a pawn shop or fast food place. I'd be in the grocery store and see a tall, dark-haired figure from the back and I'd trail up and down aisles until I got a front view to be absolutely sure it wasn't him. I'd hear noises outside the house at night and open my window, calling his name softly, or I'd go out onto the porch to see if he was there.

I tried his cell over and over but he never answered. Then I'd call just to hear his voice on the outgoing message, until eventually that was gone, too.

I drove by his old house, even knocked on the door once hoping whoever lived there would understand and let me walk through, trying to gather memories, even bad ones, and store them away so I could share them with Cameron if he ever came back.

Every day I checked the mailbox for a letter or postcard, flipping through the grocery store ads to make sure nothing was stuck in the pages. I created an e-mail news alert so that I'd know if his name was mentioned in any newspapers. Even Mom and Alan couldn't let go — Mom admitted to using her connections at the hospital to make sure he hadn't turned up sick or dead anywhere in the state; Alan was late coming home one night and confessed he thought for sure he'd seen Cameron walking out of the downtown men's shelter and onto a bus, which Alan then followed to the end of the line.

But it was never him. It was like he'd dropped off the face of the earth. It was like he'd died all over again.

One night, about three weeks after he left, I found myself awake at four a.m. thinking about him. First my thoughts were *about* him, and then they were *to* him, and soon it all became a sort of prayer — a prayer to Cameron Quick. The words were statements: *I won't forget you* and *Don't forget me* and *Whatever happens, I'm always here.* Then they were questions: *Where are you?* and *Will I ever see you again?* and *Why didn't you say good-bye?* Pretty soon I was talking right out loud, as if he were in the room with me and the thing that had lurked just beneath all my looking began, finally, to poke through the surface.

"How," I whispered, "could you leave me again?"

That question dug right into the part of me that was hurting most. Because hadn't we talked about this, all of this? The importance of our connection, what it meant to find each other again, the way it made what had happened to us and between us not be a waste, not be for nothing. He would know, he *had* to know, that not saying good-bye would be the worst end of all. I wouldn't have done that to him, ever, in a million years.

I got out of bed and went across the room to curl into the chair where he'd spent that night talking to me through the dark. I pressed my face into the upholstery and cried.

Soon there was a knock on my door — a quiet, Alan sort of knock. It was his coffee and writing time already. I wanted him to come in but couldn't manage to speak. The door inched open.

"Jenna?"

"I'm over here," I finally said, sniffling. "In the chair."

I saw his figure come closer in the dimness; he sat on the ottoman, facing me. "I don't know what to say," he said softly.

"Me, neither."

He reached over and patted my ankle. I kept my face turned into the chair. We stayed like that until my alarm clock beeped.

CHAPTER 26

THE CARD AND POINSETTIA CAME THE DAY CHRISTMAS BREAK
started. They were sitting on our porch when I got home from working out with Steph at the JCC. She and I had actually gotten closer since Cameron left. Part of it was what I'd said at the Halloween party, and her trying to prove to me that she did know me and love me anyway. Also it was like she'd seen a new side of me during that time, that I wasn't just good old dependable, predictable Jenna. I was someone who might actually have a secretly complicated life, like hers.

"The whole deal is awesomely romantic, if you think about it," she'd said at the gym that morning. "This tall, handsome man from your past remembered you all those years and looked for you and *found* you and came back and changed your life. I know it was like two months ago, but I still think about it practically every day."

Imagine how *I* feel, I thought. "It would have been more romantic if he'd managed to say good-bye," I'd said, ending the conversation by stepping into the shower.

When I pulled up to the house and saw the plant, I figured it was from one of Mom or Alan's colleagues, or the LDS ward down the street that liked to do neighborly stuff during the holidays. The outside of the card read, "For the Vaughns." I had my hands full with my gym bag and water bottle and decided to leave it for my parents to discover when they got home.

Later, Mom stood in the kitchen doorway, dressed in her scrubs and holding the plant and card. "Jenna? Did you see this?"

My hands were busy squishing together a meat loaf in progress. "Yeah. I guess I should have brought it in. Sorry."

"Honey, it's from Cameron."

I turned around, my ground turkey–covered hands suspended in midair.

"There's another card inside," she continued. "For you. He must have sent it to the florist and had them forward it." She set down the plant and came over to me. "Wash your hands. I'll finish this."

I cleaned up and took the envelope into my room; just seeing my name in his handwriting made me feel closer to him already. I was holding the envelope that had been touched by the pen that was held in his hands. I studied that for a long time — the slant of the J, the curve of the e. I opened it and unfolded the sheet of yellow legal pad paper.

Hi.

My eyes wanted to skip to the end, but I made myself read it line by line.

I've been wanting to write this for a long time but didn't know how to start. The time since I left has gone by fast. And slow, too. I came back to California. Been spending time with my brothers and sisters . . . and my mom. Decided I didn't want to put them all through any custody stuff. It would be just one more crappy thing for them to endure, you know? But I'm trying to help them all out a little so that things can maybe be different for my brothers and sisters. When I stayed with you I kept thinking how I wished they had someone like Alan. Then I thought maybe it could be me.

It was kind of selfish of me to run off from them to find you. Not that I regret that in any way, trust me, but it hit me that instead of sitting around being frustrated and angry maybe I could do something. I had enough of feeling helpless. Spent the first 16 years of my life feeling that way.

It meant leaving you, which I hated.

Good-byes are the worst.

If I didn't leave like I did I might not have gone through with it. I couldn't look you in the eye knowing I might not see you again for a long time. Sat down to write you a note but couldn't do that either. I would have drowned from all the crying — better if I didn't start.

If I could split myself in half and take part of me to CA and leave part of me in UT, I would have done it in a second. Wanted to be in both places at once, so much. But you don't need me like they do. Think about how it was for us back then and you'll understand. Anyway, you'll be fine. I have no doubt about that. You're the bravest person I know. Always have been.

But I'm sorry.

I hope everything is going great for you, Jenna. (I'm finally getting used to calling you Jenna.) You deserve all the happiness you can get.

My address is on the other side of the paper if you ever want to write to me. I understand if you don't. The one thing I promise is that from now on you'll always know where and how to find me.

Remember that no matter where I am or what I'm doing I've got a special place inside me that's all for you. It's been there since the day we met.

Love always.

Cameron

By the end of the day I had that letter memorized.

Mom, Alan, and I put together a big Christmas box to send to Cameron and his brothers and sisters. We filled it with gift cards for grocery stores and department stores, books, and homemade cookies. We included a prepaid calling card, the idea being that Cameron could call us anytime, but he didn't. Maybe he needed the minutes to take care of other stuff. I tried not to be upset about it or feel let down every time the phone rang and it wasn't him; even with his letter and apology and explanation, I still felt a pinch of hurt from time to time.

More of an ache, really, a stretching of my heart in the general direction of California.

CHAPTER 27

SOMETIMES I STILL STARE INTO SPACE AND THINK ABOUT Cameron.

I think about how there are certain people who come into your life, and leave a mark.

I don't mean the usual faint impression: *He was cute, she was nice, they made me laugh, I wish I'd known her better, I remember the time she threw up in class.*

And I don't just mean that they change you. A lot of people can change you — the first kid who called you a name, the first teacher who said you were smart, the first person who crowned you best friend. It's the change you remember, the firsts and what they meant, not really the people. Ethan changed me, for instance, but the longer we've been apart the more he sort of recedes into the distance as a real person and in his place is a cardboard cutout that says First Boyfriend.

I'm talking about the ones who, for whatever reason, are as much a part of you as your own soul. Their place in your heart is tender; a bruise of longing, a pulse of unfinished business. My mom was right about that. Just hearing their names pushes and pulls at you in a hundred ways, and when you try to define those hundred ways, describe them even to yourself, words are useless. If you had a lifetime to talk, there would still be things left unsaid.

Which is maybe why I don't write to Cameron as often as I thought I would. Every time I sit in front of the computer or put a pen to paper, I find myself in a dead stall. We talk on the phone sometimes but never quite get around to saying much of anything important until the very last two minutes of the conversation when he tells me how much it means to hear my voice, and I tell him I miss him, and we make vague promises about seeing each other again. In the back of my mind I have this idea that when I graduate I'll load up my car and drive across the wide expanse of Nevada, into California, find Cameron on the map, and knock on his front door. And we'll talk all night.

But then I don't.

The pulse of unfinished business still beats while life unfurls; days, weeks, months.

I end up going to college out of state after all, in a new place with a roommate, a person who one day I didn't know and the next day is my de facto best friend, and I'm always telling her the stories about Cameron Quick: the ring in my lunch box, escaping from his father together, chocolate chip pancakes and the time he slept in my bed and the Great Halloween Debacle of Aught Six. I don't want these memories to become slippery, to just disappear into the thin air of life the way most things seem to. I want them to stick — even the bad ones — so I repeat them often.

My roommate asks me if I'm in love with Cameron and I say no, not in love. I start to tell her that I do love him, but stop myself before it comes out. It takes some thinking; years of it, in fact. I know I said it to him that night, and I still wonder if he heard me, but as I get older I think — can it really be love if we don't talk that much, don't see each other? Isn't love something that happens between people who spend time together and know each other's faults and take care of each other? Still, by the time I've had my share of boyfriends, I discover that even the ones I truly love never bring on the same kind of feeling that I get when I think about Cameron. In the end, I decide that the mark we've left on each other is the color and shape of love. That's the unfinished business between us.

Because love, love is never finished.

It circles and circles, the memories out of order and not always complete. There's one I always come back to: me and Cameron Quick, lying on the ground in an aspen grove on a golden fall day, the aspen leaves clattering and quaking the way they do. Cameron turning to me, reaching out a small and dirty hand, which I take and do not let go.

ACKNOWLEDGMENTS

Many thanks to my wonderful editor, Jennifer Hunt, whose vision and patience pushed me further into this story than I thought I'd be able to go. Thanks, too, to T.S. Ferguson, Victoria Stapleton, Ames O'Neill, and the whole Little, Brown crew.

Major gratitude goes to my amazing agent, Michael Bourret, who continues to be a voice of cool-headed sanity in the wilds of my writerly angst. I'm also grateful for the sane voices of Tara Altebrando, Lew Hancock, and Emily Lupash, as well as those of all my smart and talented colleagues in the YA world.

Special thanks to Mark Miller, who gave me a ring in third grade and found me thirty years later. He generously granted me permission to use the memory of that ring, and the freedom to make up the rest.

As always, the biggest thanks of all goes to my husband, Gordon Hultberg, whose steadfast love and support continues to create the necessary space.